I0737629

Presumed Guilt

A novel

M. Schell

Quotes concerning priestly formation are formulated from Rev. Dennis H. Holtschneider's text of the Vincentian Formation Theory which is found on the famvin website; permission was granted.

Cover Design—MS and LS
Publisher—MS
Genre: fiction (includes crime, religion categories)
ISBN—978-0-9895511-9-9
Printed in the United States of America.
Special acknowledgment: The Write On Institute for editing.

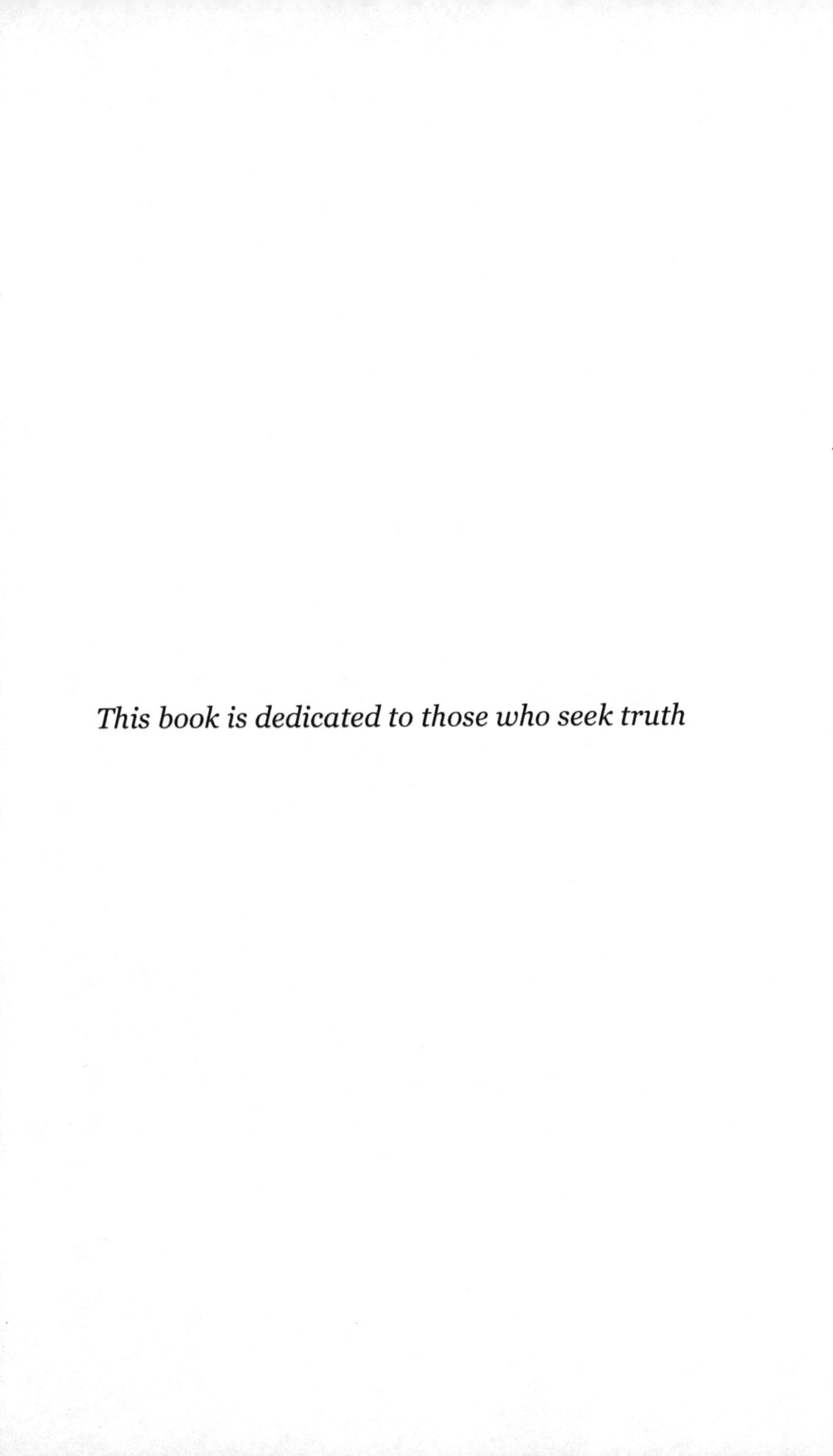

This book is dedicated to those who seek truth

Part I

Introduction

Communication is risky. Cell phones are attached to people like ribs—the Biblical rib—the one that creates a companion, a significant other. Well, I'm an exception. You see I'm partial to a particular device. The basic set-up: a box, a few knobs, the speaker, the headphones, and the antenna; all allowing high frequency voice or code transmission—a safe communication regulated by international treaty.

In the beginning, amateurs called themselves "hams"; they built sending and receiving sets for less than a monthly grocery bill. My original interest was saving lives by radio communication during natural and manmade disasters; that related closely to my work of spiritual intervention. But aside from crisis management, this device also enables friendship.

Why not use a cell phone? It's a risky device. Too easy. And destructive. You see it took one call and one situation to nearly destroy all I previously represented. I have a lot of past behind me and probably very little future ahead. I've made mistakes. But what is relevant is poor judgment. It becomes the eternal moment—or another story.

1

The Rebel

"There is something shifty about a guy with cowboy boots and a black skirt..."

It was not *what* he said, but *the way* he said it, that scratched my ear. He was an angry man with a beautiful immigrant wife and he resented my position because she could come to me most anytime. I had an open-door policy—a policy that extended to all ages. I was young. She was older, but also young, and the six years between us of less importance, because the nature of my position prevented her husband from interrupting at will.

This woman and others were welcoming my official birthday. I say "official," because in the American Midwest, five percent of the rural population have discrepancies on legal documents—the applicable one being the birth certificate made out by a drunk physician with poor memory, apparently after fatiguing deliveries on the same night. And so, during this warm welcome, the beautiful wife had pulled together comments here and there and concluded I was nearly the age of her brother. He was born in '27 and I in '30—an unluckier decade. Why unlucky? Well, it had moderately to do with economics, and more to do with the Wall Street mess, and sort of connected to my height. Yet it began with blond curly hair—at least during my childhood.

Most men are proud of their offspring, but I am a contradiction alongside my three brown hair siblings: burred brothers and a tousled sister. There is something odd about being five foot eight and slightly built when both parents are tall, sturdy, and very Bohemian. My decent father loved me. Still at intervals he studied my stature and blond hair out of the corner of his eye, and never held the medical doctor or my good mother responsible.

On the other hand, he insisted I wear cowboy boots. It rendered me two inches taller. Maybe that brought me closer to him while we worked the fields. Maybe it was supposed to make me manly. But my brothers and I were like harnessed horses—and that made it *darn hard* in the late thirties. Darn hard since the great depression. Looking back, it's possible at age nine I was too young or too self-absorbed to assimilate why families push harshly when there is less money.

Being the oldest, I had the most work, and subsequently more privileges. But I would not endure dirt with sweat. A rescue was on the horizon to the east, to the great city of St. Louis near the Mississippi River—a promising formation, an alternate to calloused hands, and also, a possible answer to my mother's prayer.

So at the end of an ordinary farm day I would stand before the mirror hanging over the porch washbowl. I'd run a wide-toothed comb through my blond wavy mop. I'd look long and hard, and part of me questioned if that reflection was cut out for preaching and teaching and solving people problems. I'd create the part I hadn't seen—a black-cassock rebel in cowboy boots roaming the land, and immediately I felt important.

Owning a seeded ego balanced by a sprouting sense of humor, now I could imagine myself solving life's complications whispered between a thin slatted screen, dividing penitent and person. Later this would prove naïve—though it allowed access to beautiful and non-beautiful women, some with disturbing husbands.

And I'm getting ahead of the mirror.

2

Small rural American communities are distinctive. Sight, sound and smells are repetitive. You don't forget narrow bridges and traffic submitting to wide grain trucks and tractor-trailers, or county roads off main highways that crunch and spin the dust, or rumbling rails and hazard warnings that say, "Don't test me." You don't forget open air dumps and large pig farms with foul odors flying with the wind, or the nasty smoke of burned rubbish that irritates sinuses and pains the eyes. Absolutely, you recall the good pleasures of late afternoon fishing with humid still air or rock tossing in a drizzling rain.

Our Kansas dairy and crop farm was midway between Bull Creek and the Missouri border. That put us eight miles from Louisburg, or "Little St. Louis," with its population of 600 plus people. The town felt small back then. It supplied a one-pump gas station, basic postal service, the grocery, and a hardware store. Also, it promoted school, social, and church activities. In the late thirties, into the forties, everything of importance in my youth seemed connected to Saturday night sports and Sunday morning Mass. That said manageable work and proper play habits could attract the designation of "altar boy."

When I took on this notable responsibility that competed with basketball and daily farm chores, there were other actions worlds away—more extraordinary than being selected for altar serving. My relatives were analyzing an aggressive Hitler who had invaded Czechoslovakia on the pretext of protecting people who lived in the western part of Bohemia, a place called Sudetenland. But these facts held no distraction for an eight going on nine-year-old. Even if our teachers skimmed over the international news, it's likely the information meant little. When you're an American kid working on a farm and shooting basketball hoops and serving Mass, that's interesting enough.

A boy's life must be lived, and a boy grows up. If I milked the cows faster than usual, my little sister would say, "That's my brother," and if I scored double digits, my dad would say, "That's my boy." And if serving at Mass, my mother would say, "That's *my* son;" to achieve this, she would methodically iron trousers, starch shirts, and ask me to polish my shoes and scrub my nails. Home lye was taken very seriously. All of this was rational. No server at Mass would dare approach his responsibility with soiled hands—the Lavabo, the washing of the celebrant's fingers, mandated a perfect assistant.

My Catholic upbringing impressed, not only "one true faith," but also a Biblical interpretation adamantly teaching externally clean and inwardly pure. The latter was most relevant to our *Holy Communion*—to faithfully receive this wondrous sacramental presence as the wafer was changed to the essence of Jesus, at the point of its consecration. It proved my respect for the "Body and Blood of Christ," even if my Protestant friends remarked, "So you're eating Jesus."

Service and church, this was the Sunday norm, but when my mother started to volunteer me for extra assignments, my father had to adjust. If any of the altar boys were ill, or had a last-minute excuse, and could not serve their assigned slot, I was pushed forward to put on the loose flowing black attire that skimmed my polished shoes, plus the pleated white cotton overtop that dropped well below the belt line. It layered my long robe.

On a particularly hurried morning, I pulled the white layer on backwards which left the hem line shorter to the posterior, indicating I didn't have it all together. My mother fidgeted during the entire Mass. As for me, the Church's ornamentation proved more distracting. The liturgy committee had recently approved the restoration of several objects and so during this incident with my faulty serving attire, I noticed the life size statue of the beautiful Mary. She had this pearly face with a smile poised to weep if I should do anything wrong. Part of me wanted to fall upon her feet and assure her that I would never hurt my mother or any woman purposefully. At the same time, I noticed the statue of St Joseph. It seemed bland compared to the other's beauty, and yet it was a positive reminder I had a job to do and should be very attentive.

At Mass there were multiple tasks and the most important required kneeling at the side of the altar, and ringing the designated *hand bell* at the *precise moment* of consecration. Profound responsibility. At age fifteen, I thought how incredible to proclaim the sacramental miracle. This day and every day after of altar serving, my bent knees would go cold and my clean grip would turn hotter than an arduous round on a basketball court.

Even with church responsibilities, it was sports that rewarded adolescent development and clarified my future vision of life. Teamwork requires attentive strategy. Attentive players will promote optimum results. My defensive skills were effective, but my scoring skills were not advancing. Maximizing potential is incredibly important. Possibilities surged when the coach discovered my visual impairment; mother took the coach's observation to heart and insisted on heavy dark frames—the kind withstanding aggressive school sports or rugged outdoor chores. Just like that: things changed. My offensive contributions reflected on the scoreboard, and at home, life transformed.

For better or worse I could see clearly, and my ego was threatened. I didn't like the peering pimples in the mirror. I didn't like the "four-eyed" jokes from my siblings. My blond hair looked lighter and I felt shorter. My younger brothers seemed taller than they had the week before. My little sister seemed plump with her tighter fitting clothes. My father looked serious with his durable overalls, and mother looked cheerless in her faded paisley dress. Regardless, I needed my eyewear.

Then, during a mid-season away game, the basketball knocked my heavy frames across the gym, and cracked the glass lens. I was upset—no, actually I was doomed. At home, my mother and father discussed the future. "I can't buy that boy a new pair glasses every three weeks," he puffed from cigarette purple lips. And then came her affirmative, "I understand."

Soon after, church and altar serving was appointed "a lot safer," and I was at the beck and call of the local pastor. Simultaneously, my chores increased. I was back to milking and milking, bucket after bucket, and I saw no end to washing teats, swishing tails, and scooping manure. But my new vision with a cracked lens had a way of directing me, and with the sparseness of income and my father's dairy struggle, it pointed to another future. At sixteen and a half, I convinced my pastor that I was called to his honorable vocation—a reputable vocation. He agreed to help me explore my options.

3

One can be terribly young at seventeen to be making a decision. Why a priest in the family? My pacifist father ignored me—no arguing. He felt disillusionment from World War II, and he didn't want to fight anyone—not with four children, the demanding cows, and a recuperating farm. My mother was supportive; her approval would eventually lead to a minor seminary under the Archdiocese of St. Louis.

Taking the train across Missouri, I arrived in St. Louis, and then took city transport to an unincorporated area on the southwest limits of the county. My placement would start as a high school junior in a crowded dorm as out of sorts as one could imagine, because institutional transition was evolving. The Archbishop Ritter was closing the Latin High School and establishing two programs: four years of high school and two years of college, and, two years of college and four years of theology.

While many disliked the tighter census and lack of order and unpredictability, support came from a kind and very cheerful mentor. He would say, "The best learning is grounded in real life and real situations." That included crowded dorms. I had good roommates with most of them sincerely dedicated, but I concentrated on the full group—like we had done in basketball. Back then and now, we were being taught to consider the greater dimensions of our commitment.

Twenty-one months later, I would enter the first level of the college program with the emphasis on basic study foundation. Declining Washington University (privately endowed) and Saint Louis University (run by the Jesuits, predicting to go co-ed), I felt the minor seminarian college environment allowed me a priority focus. No women, just men, and also, we had excellent teachers and the flexibility for extensive community involvement. My calendar was filled with numerous inner city field trips and service outreach; and after two years, I had more exposure to those "real life" situations.

With my studious position advancing (the last two years of college to be combined with four additional years of theology at the major seminary), our elderly mentor informed us that our seminarian study would be unique. He incorporated the Vincentian philosophy. It began with a "go-then" introduction. Teaching priestly formation was not a classroom or book or lecture. It was "a ministry deeply rooted in the lives of the poor," and he would define for us the first step: "*Go* serve, *then* come back, and talk about it."

The next week, the gray-haired mentor gathered our group after an intense inner city project, where we had participated in a "big brother program" that supported teenagers with special needs. He cracked a few jokes, and then like the best of coaches or the best of teachers, he declared, "We form each other—that is, we tell our stories of success, defeat, ideals, frustrations..." Before anyone could relate this extended instruction to our recent field experience, he stated, "As we teach each other and support each other, good humor will assist us along the way."

Humor? I found this thought amazing. In walking the footsteps of others, entering in their lives, we needed a way to replenish our spirit. How else do we do this? As if reading my mind, our mentor took it farther, and with a brilliant wide grin aimed in my direction, he continued, "See to your needs." And then like a huge leap, regarding all of us, he expounded, "You'll be no good to your people if you don't take care of yourself. Cynical, burned out, frustrated people are distant from God...learn to pray...learn to reflect... Your heart needs to be fully alive...balance the demands with rest and fun."

After our subsequent years of advanced study and community service, a few of us would take "fun" too literally. We designed an escapade to a river bar on the Mississippi. Living on the dorm's second floor, we thought to tie a couple of sheets and lower our bodies cautiously. There was no dog or guard to alert the staff. Returning through an unlocked door at dusk was easy, but a late return would demand an ingenious plan: to re-enter the curfew secured entrance, a willing co-conspirator would have to borrow the keys and place them in a hidden spot. Daring, but not successful.

This venture did not imply reactive behavior to abnormal expectations. Our lives were meaningful with the seminarian emphasis placed on community outreach, it just meant, we were "normal young men" thirsty for a small rebellion. Nonetheless, we needed to examine our "acting out." When the staff discovered the infraction, they recommended a short period of alternate theological studies, the hope being to instill a sense of awe and order in our lives. In this time of booming seminarian numbers with a particular shortage of dorms in the St. Louis area, we were fortunate to be offered a probationary summer at St. Benedict's Abbey in Atchison, Kansas.

A bit of fear and self-examination did not harm us. We were programmed for poverty, chastity, obedience, and balance (or stability), and now must accept "discipline"—the experimental blend of Vincentian and Benedictine. With many institutions holding maximum numbers, the staff could screen out the half-hearted. Some of us speculated why God was calling young men in such droves. One possible conclusion: the seminarian fervor could relate to an American draft and residual fear following an unresolved Korean War.

And so led a summer of analysis... There are common ideas about attraction to the priesthood: an overly possessive mother-child relationship where the parent believes no woman would ever be deserving of her son, the situation where a young man has minimal desires (perhaps a deficit in sexual hormones), a biological chromosome factor, or the person with a confused identity caused by an over-controlling father who has taught him that women can never be trusted. The "calling" could also be the manipulative desire for a high position as to exert strong influence over a large population. And perhaps the most revolutionary reason attracting young men to the priesthood was a desire to change the past and test the future.

Many of us were escaping or recreating something and yet held a genuine belief we would draw nearer to God if we served Him well. Ultimately, our Benedictine experience would promote discipline and selfless virtues—something equivalent to a soldier for Christ, rather than a soldier for one's country.

With our three months completed, we were back in St. Louis to enjoy our return and the changing leaves. Autumn announced a full year left in our vocation formation. Checking the community mailbox, there was a note from our older mentor. His shaky handwriting emphasized, "It's not over till it's over. The poor make you Vincentian! You serve the poor, and then you ask why it has to be this way— and then, begin to read sociology, economics, social work, psychology, substance abuse, history, politics, government, housing, nutrition, health, management, spirituality..." Read and read. Was he reminding us of our last year of studious responsibility? No. I suspected this year was insufficient, and we would keep on learning.

During class, on the second day back from the disciplinary experience, our mentor described a working relationship to God so magnificently that I would envy the beauty exuding from this old priest who seemed to profoundly love his profession. I grasped hope for the most inadequate as he went on to say, "There is always room to grow. The gap between God and ourselves can be made closer." I took from his words, that in working with the physically poor and the poor in spirit, there was always more to understand. And yet, he reminded us that we should pace even this. "Life lessons will come in rushes and stalls. Talk about it. Ask what works and doesn't work." Our mentor would re-emphasize that formation is not something compacted for delivery once and for all time. *It's not over till it's over...*

4

An emerging world awaited us. A change of attitudes had carried over from World War II and the Korean War (the latter never formally ended), and new attitudes were persisting. Like many men (priests, military, or otherwise), I was questioning and/or adapting. Also women were realizing their importance. Conflict had brought greater feminine awareness—mothers and daughters had been given a limited but unforgettable slot of equal opportunity, and going back to the "old ways" was not popular. McCormick and Sanger were organizing safer health care delivery, and others were pushing women rights in the workplace. Advantage and capability should walk together. Resistance to the woman's voice from within the Church endured, and this and other problems contributed to a particular level of internal institutional stagnation.

It was the mid-fifties. I had a limited break to visit family, a routine for the last ten years, since leaving home at seventeen. We were outside on the porch and my sister was trying to decide what college she should attend and was asking for advice. With his other children, Dad had never gotten too involved. He believed young people had multiple choices and high school counselors were hired to assist their process. I tried to stay out of it until my sister's frustration became obvious. Dad was treating her just like us, and yet she *wanted* his advice. It would have been simple to conclude girls are weak and therefore "need our help," but suddenly I entered into a different mindset.

If I had more female siblings for comparison, some may have exerted greater independence, and others less. My sister is who she is—this is not based on gender but on personhood. If she wanted Dad's advice, that was OK. Along my track of maturing, I was examining a singular communication and relating its unique value to understanding humanity: women and men deserve equal respect regardless of what approach they use in problem solving or tilling. This reality was not something emphasized in my seminarian formation.

In the future ahead, the Church's attitude toward women was bound to irritate: women were boxed in with stereotypical limits. Having been a dairy farmer's son, raised with male and female often tasking together, the Catholic Church's discrimination would fester. My sister had not desired a leadership position, but others do. Priestly exclusion of these women cuts out influential input (possible exceptions—mothers of priests, or rich old ladies).

Once I started with my first assignment in the Kansas City diocese, de-programming began. Forget that Vincentian stuff about the "balance" of service and rest. Place your nose to the air and get a good sniff and stop smelling joy and drop the humor and pick up your shovel and dig up the sins and bury the evil; and supposedly the inner city offered the dirtiest hole as we were repetitively warned against predatory tendencies of the opposite sex.

Soon I prioritized my independence for community work, especially my interest in neglected or dysfunctional families; but the local bishop had specific rules outlined for new priests: keep regular contact with male support, hire relatives for personal housekeepers, travel with a protective companion, serve the poor but never alone, offer daily Mass, be weary of confessions of excessive detail, and above all—beware of beautiful women. And to encourage a safe living arrangement, the bishop held up our Holy Father as the primary role model.

The Pope had held his office for less than two decades. Past war times and negativity were hushed. The neglect of Czechoslovakian Catholics had meant loss of education and freedom, which voided their individualism; the horror of Hitler had been swept under archival shelves. Instead, the "Pope's saving of the Vatican" and "his public criticism of satanic Nazism" had been highlighted. Now, the increasingly frail Pius XII had a stern German housekeeper known as Madame Lehnert; she was protecting him from a controversial past. She limited his contacts. Often he took meals alone. The Pope expounded, "Communing singularly leads to pure thought."

Among many, Pope Pius XII was seen as a saintly man. Of course the general public could not guess how quietly he enjoyed his big Cadillac, gifted by the elevated Cardinal Spellman—a powerful man frequently referred to as the "American Pope." This favored situation was well known in European circles; apparently, Madame Lehnert allowed private audiences with Spellman, and gossip flew about. An aspiration to future pope-hood may have looked tempting to some religious. Not me. Even the thought of elevation turned me sour.

In America, the rebels were gathering. One could see potential problems. I migrated toward the progressive theology in the Jesuit elements, challenging papal boundaries. In my vision, the Pope's face of the Holy Catholic Church, felt sometimes archaic. Historically, he had insisted on central control and universal authority, having moral and ethical rule over most aspects of society, seeking powerful influence—this reflected in forty some encyclicals, almost a thousands addresses and radio broadcasts. As for political views, he was openly severe; he made no secret of his attitude toward the United Nations, claiming that any authentic peaceful organization could not trace its origin to war. His basic message: The Church must avoid the downfall of compromise. Hesitantly, the question rose—did I, as a priest, have a *proper* allegiance to the church's highest representative?

Catholics had been diverse for years. (Ethiopian element particularly sited.) African elements were evolving. Interdenominational collaborations and international links were evident. All this loudly recognized, even as the aging Pope was referring to Protestants as heretical and Greek Orthodox as schismatic and blatantly posting he was not open to easing his profound authority. I asked again: Was this my church?

5

The Test

So here I was, Father Jakob Schieli (Father Jake, for short) recently ordained and having serious doubts. A weekend away was requested—to connect with my previous mentor. His wrinkled old face exerted light. "When you are weak, remember your history." I assumed he was referring to the intense formational study of Saint Vincent DePaul—and probably so—but he elaborated, "Wisdom is learned from studying the lives of others; we learn from their mistakes...and still we must figure out *on our own* because the world changes... You are the church, your people are the church—go, serve them!"

Armed with love and understanding, I returned to Kansas City, spiritually motivated to give my all and soon was appointed associate pastor to a poor city parish. Like Saint Louis, there were problems with prostitution, drugs and homelessness, expressions of loss of faith and hope. Standard goals were placed aside. Instead, *I must walk the walk; I must enter into their lives*. I sought a team. Evaluations were mandated—one of which I kept to myself: If I ever had a parish of my own I could trust women and nuns.

Women are the true workers in the church, the lights that shine. I do not demean men. But like corporate America, the church coveted its tiers of place and appointment. Then Mrs. Juwel walked through our office like a cardinal—not like flashy species among trees—but the kind of person a good church *should* produce. She worked with an organization that procures legal services and defense representation for those who cannot afford otherwise. This was a valuable contact. We had poor families who needed her type of legal assistance. With attentive listening, I learned another story—an interesting background: Nearly a hundred years ago, Mrs. Juwel's maternal ancestor (Edward Salmon, a Prussian born lawyer) began what was known as the Legal Aid Society; its original focus on immigration rights. Their motto had proclaimed no barriers to nationality; the organization believed when people are treated justly and are protected they will be loyal to their new country.

Mrs. Juwel was a reflection of her maternal ancestor; she surrounded herself with migrants, immigrants, and the general poor. She loved children. Her greatest desire and asserted goal: the constitutional right for children to counsel, at government expense. An undercurrent was rolling with plans to take the issue to the Supreme Court. I had no problem visualizing this Catholic woman bringing passion and influence to many causes.

There was another light in the church. I enjoyed a friendship with Sister Rose Marie—at least twenty years my senior. This energetic nun possessed the heart of the Sisters of Charity. Here stood an unforgettable person. She introduced her methods of seeking outside assistance for the poor: enlisting a strong group of volunteers, organizing fundraising programs, and growing outreach. I had an immediate connection as her order followed the traditions of Vincent de Paul.

Sister Rose Marie honored our founder, the patron saint of charitable organizations—remembered by the laity for his great assistance to the marginalized. She disclosed her ideal of teamwork, tying Vincent de Paul to Louise de Marillac—a testimony of gifted women and men succeeding together. (To explain: Louise, a widow with a son, had a concern for health care, hospitals and orphans. Vincent, a peasant turned priest, served colleges, missions and "home sites" like France, Piedmont, Poland and Madagascar. In these endeavors, the priest aided Louise and vice versa.)

Another person I worked with, the pragmatic business minded Sister Mary Margaret (also a friend of Sister Rose Marie), offered this side note: Beyond the work with the Vincentians and the Sisters of Charity, the great seventeenth century patron saint had intervened for the English Benedictine Sisters order—an odd coincidence with my short "discipline" exposure to the Benedictines in Atchison. Sister Mary Margaret would re-enter my life in later years. She was truly steady. I should have chosen her for my lifelong mentor; her wisdom and judgment would have guided me well, and perhaps saved me from myself.

As I spent more time around these impressive women, it became apparent I lacked the public boldness of Mrs. Juwel, and the endless energy of Sister Rose Marie, and the serious business sense of Sister Mary Margaret. Being different, I was one to listen often, simmer quietly, and delegate as necessary. The world needs all personality types, and this experience with "workers" pressed the belief in a future church that should expand the opportunities for women. This conclusion was reinforced by observing many smart and talented women laboring to make parishes function. If something needed to be done expediently, they would do it. The face of the church is traditionally male, but the hands and spirit are more often women.

Then and now, women deserve recognition, advancement, and paid positions. This isn't to say the parish or a larger body must employ or salary everyone. An organization has to deal with their limitations. Communities thrive with selfless service. But volunteers should represent *all lives*, not the Catholic approach—that targets bright women, and especially nuns—as the lowest order of the church.

6

By 1960, my particular intellectual circle was greatly inspired by Pope John the XXIII, the old man with young ideas. One of the most critically promoted points since the first great council was the re-evaluation of the papacy position. Meanwhile, the local bishop was moving my physical body on to an independent assignment to serve divided parishes in our rural diocese.

I saw no connection to this new assignment and my short history of inner city poverty or social work. Inwardly I accepted it; but outwardly allowed an inch growth of my blond hair, exchanged my heavy rimmed eyewear for a less bold pair, and replaced my thick cassock—still worn over dark slacks and a dark shirt with the identifying collar—for a lighter garment easily rolled under my arm. To offer priestly support, the weekly men's group at the Jesuit College was less than ten miles away. Probably not the bishop's preference, but I intended to stay connected with ecumenical dialogue.

As our new progressive Pope advanced the Vatican II process, and its important agenda, I was anxious to get started with local matters. Defining the dual parish terrain, I drove about the dusty countryside separating my two assigned communities, covering a radius of nearly twenty miles. Finding crops and cattle felt familiar. They marked a return to farmland and country roots. Visualizing more down time, I considered a roaming hobby; so later I purchased a secondhand guitar, and without hesitation, bought new leather highs seeing nothing odd about cowboy boots with a black cassock.

But an ooze of past demise came to my awareness after settling in: the original church building—which seated five hundred—met its end years ago. First, the priest *rectory* was burned down, challenging previous resistance, and signaling a community mandate to dynamite the large impressive church in order to create two small serviceable parishes. So fifty years later, I moved into this competitive region.

The first community in my rural assignment had a two-story parish house/part-time office center with the upstairs designated as my personal quarters. The building adjacent was divided into a chapel, parochial classrooms, and a small private area for the teaching religious (three nuns). On the same property the church owned a multi-purpose building—constructed on the original intended foundation for a larger church. Since the Catholic population never expanded, the lower area was designated for a stage and school gym with the upper structure promoting more activity space.

The second serving parish was fifteen minutes away—or even a bit more distant on the unpredictable weathering of back roads. This community had a freestanding simple church structure—straightforward with no futuristic plans—and a small gathering space. No parochial school. Their children participated in the public system, in the same town as the Jesuit College.

Two parishes. I drew a plan and formulated several strategies. I would need to organize strong youth groups and coordinate multiple events to improve community relationships. To decrease competition, I didn't want people burning my rectory, there would be equal Sunday service time and quality presence to both communities—a bit complicated with one having a parochial school and the other not.

Admitting my limited assistive experience to a Kansas City Catholic elementary, my confidence rested with the three nuns. Delegate. Step back. Observe. Inevitably, I would feel more tied to my residential parish with its parochial program but would keep this to myself.

7

The Church exploded. Metaphorically. After my welcome to the community and carefully planned strategies for balance and fairness, newspapers were describing a revolution. I had been following it. Pope John XXIII was still leading the Vatican Council. The "universal church" was moving from Latin to allow colloquial languages, so our services were to be in English with the priest facing the people (previously his back to the people, as the altar stood before him). The communion rail—that divided celebrant from the people—would be recycled. The laity (male and female) would be allowed to participate in liturgy. Women could actually be lectors and even serve the holy elements. Many were half committed. Others were excited. Change was real. For some, the upheaval was scary.

The great resisters called the Holy Father "a devil in lamb clothing" or referred to his movement as "devil's work." This didn't slow down the progressive parishes. I set about to lead our communities: more modifications and liturgical music that sounded high-spirited and motivational. Strict fasting and severe rules were now revised—less outward witness, more internal. Were Catholics becoming Protestant? The anxieties were deep. Gone were the Latin cadences. No more Ave Maria? The major critics claimed the church had dismissed its own history. The extremists described a Catholic holocaust. And yet, parish families were acclimating.

Perhaps the east and west coasts would adjust faster, but rural Kansas had its own pace. Thank God, I had a supportive group behind me. Still problems were obvious. Money was tight. Some were reducing their tithing. Others were "active agents"—watching every move, consulting their new printed editions of Conciliar Vatican documents and reporting any minute deviation to the affiliated diocesan bishop. Our local representative cautioned me to slow down with the new Vatican directives. I had been enthused but pulled back, and put the emphasis on the Confraternity of Christian Doctrine (CCD) program. My young people needed consistent education, leading the way to the future.

These special youth meetings were reinforced by outdoor prayer groups and hootenannies—the latter being campfire gatherings with folk guitar and voices ringing "There is a Season" or "All Over This Land." And when the right season arrived, the parish team instigated adult discussion clubs to emphasize the message of Vatican II—hoping to win over older hearts and gain expansive unity. Still, the spy-agents and outsiders moved farther to the right, and that included the man with the beautiful wife.

I could never figure him out. He was a college educated second-generation Irish farmer firmly planted among the predominantly German-Bohemian community. His mouth was handsome and loud; he was weather tanned, opinionated and flirted excessively with other women. It did not make him popular with the husbands. He owned the most land, had the largest family, and insisted his children be the bold ones in the front pews. (Yes, pews plural. A dozen well-dressed youngsters will easily occupy Sunday front rows in a small church.)

I was not impressed. From his children's confessions, I gathered he was overbearing and sometimes very cruel—almost predicting rebellion. One of his sons revealed a remorseful desire to do harm. And from the spousal confession—and yes, voices could be identified—she feared she could not please him sufficiently. I concluded he preferred his wife pregnant without relief. I almost pitied her, and then the Pope declared he was putting "Sexual Ethics" and "The Christian Family" on his agenda, and soon my door was open to *anyone* who needed counsel.

Then my hopeful world took a terrible blow. Pope John XXIII died. He had been ill for a long time and few realized it. The Vatican Council was still in progress and another would be elected quickly. Our community's extremist Irish farmer saw the Pope's passing as a divine sign. In this small rural area, there were probably others with the same viewpoint. Praise to Mary, our Holy Mother—giving her my intercessory credit—the succeeding Pope Paul VI had a democratic spirit. However, among political and powerful forces, the new leader appeared unable to remedy the "absolutist" papal controversy while the council continued to study and review the tradition of priest celibacy and hierarchy.

During the ongoing Vatican sessions, one teaching remained highly contentious: contraception. By 1965, I had Wednesday and Saturday confessions full of confused women. For years, many had been taught that any form of birth control was sinful. I had always thought this teaching quite severe. Now it was being discussed with feverish energy. It seemed impossible to draw a workable solution between natural and artificial methods. The so-called "right intention" was being tossed around. In the confession, I stuck to my general advice—*personal conscience must be the highest guide—even above church mandates.*

Discussion of body and "natural" and inconsistent interpretations made people anxious. Medical science was moving fast and I didn't believe the council should create another "Galileo Affair." But the debate went on, and it would split practicing Catholics. In the end, the council left the birth control issue hanging. The decision would affect the institution indefinitely.

8

Vatican Council II came to a close. Soon after something moved or pushed me to have my eyes re-examined. Maybe subconsciously there was hope for another spectacular vision of the church. The specialist recommended contacts: "It will slow your visual decline." OK. Sounded wise. I was thirty-six. I had been a priest for nine years; I had been with the rural people for two-thirds of those years, and had morphed from the formal Father Jakob Schieli to the familiar "Father Jake." My past St. Louis inner circle teased me, "Oh, contacts—another new image—next you'll be leaving us all!"

Actually, it wasn't amusing. A significant number of friends were leaving the priesthood. For a few, the external Vatican II transformation had happened too fast—perhaps irreverently. And for others the internal church had not progressed far enough. Example: The celibacy issue. Historically, the church tolerated married priests in the Eastern Church—so why not the Latin Church?

Though programmed "once a priest, always a priest"—amazingly, the Pope would give "official" permission to a vast number to exit the ministry.

Public justifications were: factors of antiquated formation (the admission of very young candidates who did not understand the depth of their vows), or factors of certain techniques or stifled discussions (likely a result of Pius XII autocratic control, top down), or the general lack of adequate preparation. The Jesuits were among the exceptional: they were armed with values and sophistication that supported strength and commitment to their vocation.

Wisdom is learned from studying lives. "And still there is much we have to figure out on our own because the world changes." These last words kept me awake at night. It felt like predestination. Being young, I wanted to understand it all quickly, and I tried to sympathize with the celibacy controversy even when treasuring my own vows. Regardless of numerous viewpoints (some respected), one seemed most clear: celibacy did not negate my manhood. Chastity did not make me less of a sexual being. When I compared human marriage and its physical way of "speaking" love (a very good love that takes joy in another's existence), my celibacy had its own spoken love—it held God as the "other" and thus I vowed to lose my life in this other.

During an anticipated gathering of peer support, our consensus stated any sacred love, married or priestly, is a sacrament, a powerful force, a love inspired by the Holy Spirit. But one of my friends proposed that physical human love was potentially divine, though if misinterpreted, such sound blasphemous. He claimed if we had more canonized married saints (not widow or widowers), perhaps the hierarchy would be inspired to understand the potential of sexual expression; maybe this would promote the idea of marriage in the ministry. Still I struggled with his theory. Though I may have disagreed, the idea was not criticized.

Even as I meditated weeks later, I turned restless. A break was essential. I had finished packing a light bag, and was fixing a thermos of coffee, when one of the nuns popped in to stay longer than either of us intended. She started with a mild tirade about the *excessive focus* on priestly problems and made it clear that the religious women had their issues. The more she talked the more she seemed to be going in circles. I accepted her frustration with the fifth and sixth grade students, with the teachers' congested space, with the musical liturgy representing inconsistencies, with a lack of privacy. Soon my effort to absorb the rambling was wearing down. Breathe deep. Here was a nun who needed a large support group. And she needed a rest!

As I mentally sought to define practical interventions, it dawned on me that *I had not been listening—I mean, really listening*. She was trying to spell out her rationale to leave the convent. Finally, she blurted out "I am sexually frustrated!" Good Lord. I had heard comments like this in the confessional, but not by a nun sitting beside me as we shared a thermos of coffee. Then "bang," as she leaned over to stamp her lips over mine, the front door opened and closed loudly—our brief moment interrupted. Someone had entered the front entry having a perfectly aligned view of us in the sitting room, and then had suddenly disappeared. I rose and delicately guided the nun out the door.

A smack on the lips. Nothing sloppy or wet. This could be taken as an impulse. Easily. A few respite days put the situation in better perspective. Affectionate hugs from parish members are a normal part of any passionate service. Warmth and sincerity from people is appreciated. Sometimes tact is necessary to steer a few emotional attachments to an acceptable substitute. I didn't see solid alternatives for this nun and felt uncomfortable being her mentor. She needed to connect with an understanding person—someone like Sister Rose Marie who had broad exposure to people and problems. I would make that happen and leave her in this woman's spiritual hands.

For me, the nun situation remained very uncomfortable. I made a choice: requested a transfer to another parish. Such would materialize twelve months later, but the nun's transfer would occur within weeks—directly after the school year finished. This normalcy would not arouse suspicion or judgment. And yet the Superior of Leavenworth's Mother House with the Sisters of Charity may have drawn her own conclusions. She would inform me that teaching assignments for small rural schools were becoming increasingly difficult, inferring our community school had a limited life.

I was perturbed and then I was not. This problem

had nothing to do with a troubled nun; it appeared our parochial school closure had been on the radar for some time—our local program was scheduled to end within two years. Even though our children were being served by selfless commitment, with laborious efforts of dedicated nuns, the present program was a drain on our parish finances. More importantly, these intelligent women deserved better living conditions and decent salaries. Very few lived with amenities. Broad picture: simply unjust. I found myself thinking, "All right sisters, go onward."

But as for the relocated nun, concern remained. That day in the rectory was partly my fault. From my viewpoint, I had failed her. Had I not been tired, I would have been present with the listening ear that exemplifies love. Perhaps this would have led to an accurate evaluation of emotions. But feelings can trap us—trap us in ourselves. Our feelings are a gift from God but we can't live for them. Had she reacted on feelings? I assume if we'd been less tired, we would have communicated clearly. She could have challenged my assessments and that's fine—anytime. It leads to dialogue and more listening. This failure was a good lesson for me. Service and rest are essential. I was reminded that I'm no good at my work, I'm no good for my people, if I don't take care of myself.

9

Evaluation

During the past six summers, parish work exemplified a different temperature and slower pace. When the parochial program dismissed every May, this offered more hours available to my *second* community—the one located closer to the Jesuit College. This small town held a similar rural outlook, but as a whole was probably more stubborn than the other. They were harder to read. A person had to rely on gut interpretation. This is my simple evaluation: the old lived for the young and those in between trusted in this value. So, the community sports program remained central, youthful tribulation and love sought advice, scandal attempted cover-up, and depending on who was related to who—people took sides.

Like an old fruit tree, the elders were rather nourishing, unless rotten apples dropped to the ground. The middle age group was adequately employed but kept their eyes on the doings of the kids. Very few people were rich, and more were borderline struggling, but the large majority had basic necessities and saved for their annual family vacations. And similar to my childhood, for many, sports and God had a competing focus.

In planning any youth related religious activities during the school year, I had counted on our Wednesday evening slot—the same evening other denominations held Bible study, discussion groups, and diverse prayer meetings. But all was difficult with this community, so unsurprising. June through August appeared "time off from mid-week events" as well as school. The only social program looked to be coffee and doughnuts following Mass. Over the last six years, I had maximized my presence by officiating the last weekend service in this parish. During coffee hour, I'd make table rounds to get better acquainted with the community. That way, when the inevitable crisis arrived, I was prepared for ministering.

But the chronic situations were harder. One of the challenges was interfaith marriage. With the nearby public school setting, more youth were exposed to interdenominational date mixing—or at least that's what we believed. We were not going to change their emotions. For those considering a life commitment, the church favored dialogue (extensive pre-marital classes) and allowed only a simple Catholic service for the public exchange of vows. The formal Mass was seen as irrelevant for those of mixed faith since intercommunion was denied—to the family, it was a penalty, and ultimately a contradiction.

This was to be my last summer. Neither of the two communities was aware of change ahead. The days passed with the usual wedding and funeral stresses and then moved into the new school year with the parochial parish situation. On the first September Sunday, I had a great sermon prepared with words from my seminarian mentor: "Life holds successes and defeat, ideals and frustrations...we will meet many along the way...and we will teach one another..." I explained, "There are no shortcuts but our final goal is peace, and peace is love—love is a certainty that we'll never be alone..." The church congregation was incredibly quiet; not an infant cried, not a child whined. I noticed the family in the front rows—then I had a double take. The man's beautiful wife was neither pregnant nor holding a baby. How had that slipped by me? Perhaps she had taken my advice two years ago—*the priority of personal conscience*. I wished her peace. I wished us all peace.

After the Mass, there was the usual exit line, everyone making the choice to shake hands, extend a blessing or ask "how was your week" or just scoot through quickly with "have a good day." The last in line was Ann, the oldest child of the strict Irish man. She seemed to be in charge of a squirmy sibling and still managed a smile—and then her typical, "Thank you, Father Jake—I liked the sermon."

Today she looked more mature. I was stepping back six years in time, when I had first met her mother— the beautiful woman. Their physical likeness grabbed me. The younger had been slightly competitive in parochial school and church programs, sometimes overly sensitive, but not unusual. And today? Something different. She wore no glasses. (Forgot them at home?) Do simple modifications make profound impressions? It was possible.

Not that long ago, I had converted to contact lenses. The high school students had been more attentive like a generational barrier was dropped. At the time I had not associated change of eyewear with anything in particular, but now I pondered about the fifteen year old—a girl with a determined smile and a hand grasping tightly on the toddler beside her.

A week passed. One of the teaching nuns approached me, stating Ann wanted to enter the convent after her sophomore year. My thoughts sped fast. The troubled religious sister, who had left our parish, had once revealed she had entered her order at age fourteen—not unusual. Many of us had entered seminarian high school at or before age sixteen; and now it seemed all too young. Considering Ann and other experiences, I discouraged it, "Tell her that she should finish school and at least two semesters of college before such an important path." The nun agreed. The subject was dropped

Mid-September, Ann had resumed wearing her glasses; she seemed everywhere—a real pleasure. She volunteered for the church choir, assisted with church cleaning, and seemed increasingly helpful with mentoring the entry level students in CCD classes and their required participation in our liturgical program. I felt young and old around her. Here I was twenty-one years her senior and she brought me delight. At times she giggled like a little girl as she whispered instructions to those under her attentive direction. At other times she had a far away look that seemed to covet the impossible.

Having always felt safe with married women and nuns (even the overly demonstrative in the rectory), I realized a particular enjoyment of the older juniors and seniors in my religious education classes. It felt very balanced. So there was no logical reason I should be dwelling specifically on young Ann, but she was interrupting my thoughts too often. Would it be convincing to say there was a concern for her wellbeing? A concern inflated because she wanted to enter a religious order? Regardless, I made a definitive effort to disperse my attention. And yet that increased Ann's effort to be exceptional.

10

October through November, as I waited for transfer news, Ann sat closer to me during our youth events. She asked permission to follow the daily chaplet of Divine Mercy. She never missed Saturday confessions—confessing sins that were not sins. Once she sought permission to see me at the rectory—a problem at home.

What's wrong? "I do all my chores but I want to earn money—babysitting—Dad says no." Why no? "I'll be out late and he won't allow the children's father to drive me home; say's he doesn't trust men." Solution? A suggestion, "The mother of the children could bring you home." She tilts her head and pushes up her eyewear, "Dad says married women shouldn't be out late either." I assure Ann that I will talk to the mother. But, out of curiosity, I ask Ann what she needs the money for. "Sunday collection." Mm-m-m... We would work out a "paid sum" for doing church tasks—a win-win.

Now with Ann taking vestments and altar cloths to laundry and iron at home, she would return them faithfully. The mother would sit with a half dozen younger ones packed in their station wagon (a three seated vehicle); she seemed occupied with a flyswatter and a magazine while her daughter never took more than ten minutes to remake the altar. Sporadically, I'd quietly step in the vestibule to see Ann running her palms over the altar cloth surface as if to smooth out invisible wrinkles, and then pull slightly on the cloth corners to finally step back and examine one side and then the other as if to check the perfection of it all.

One Saturday, the station wagon was absent. Ann was alone; we sat in the pew and visited a bit. Her mother had run home quickly as they had forgotten one vestment. This unusual moment began as a mild exchange. Ann spoke minimally and then listened to my explanation for the upcoming Christmas program. Surprisingly, she offered advice—somewhat bold. Our parish had been enlisting only girls in the holiday choir—a habit from pre-Vatican days. She thought it should be mixed. "Boys can sing too." I was well aware of the point made—she was emphasizing we need to break another local stereotype. But how does one convince the rural fellows that an inclusive choir is a stronger choir. I never succeeded. But Ann was not deterred—she loved to sing and continued her full participation.

Finally, the transfer appointment: my new parish assignment would be announced from the pulpit, January of 1967. Many in the congregation were shaking their heads with sadness or questionable frowns. As I explained the future transfer to a larger parish, about fifty miles away, I glanced at Ann. It was an unavoidable glance with her family routinely situated in the front rows. Tears were streaming down her soft face—for that single moment, I felt as cruel as the actions of her dad. She wouldn't talk to me for a month. Maybe she was just embarrassed. I waited for her voice in confession. Nothing. Before I left, I posted my new address in the bulletin. During the elaborate farewell event, Ann asked if she could visit or write me. In a generic response, I answered something about enjoying letters from all. I couldn't miss the flash of pain in her eyes.

So the young Ann was infatuated with me! Unfairly I did not take any blame. Indeed I would shrug it off. My thought was self-centered: With a long priestly career ahead, there may be many "Ann's." I was thinking each one should be released if I was to be a priest for many.

11

I adjusted my single day off to explore my soon-to-be new parish. Taking the main highway north, then a straight turn west with a small sharp bend back south, the location of the one square mile township with a red top water tower, was not complicated. The mid-size town appeared to value preservation sites, a small grocery, essential schools, a nice little park, and an old library; the last proved a good resource. Their statistics reported a population that had slowly dwindled from fourteen hundred to nine hundred and ninety, with a percentile portion contributed to thirty-two men who had lost their lives in World War II; the librarian clarified with patriotic pride that no other town in the United States had lost more soldiers per capita of population. Other data: The community had 98 percent white, with spotted minorities of Hispanic and Native American. Their mixture was similar to what I would be leaving, except the Catholic census was three times higher.

A "thank you" was expressed to the helpful librarian; and then my tight coat wrap and ear muffed exploration proceeded to locate the solid limestone building called Holy Family Church, nearly equal in height and width to the Presbyterian church. The two structures were only a few hundred feet apart. Before I could mount the steps and test the Holy Family entry doors, I bumped into an elderly person on a narrow worn bench well bundled up well for the March chill. The old man claimed to be a member of the "one true church" and commented that the Presbyterians were dwindling and the Baptists were taking over. Few questions followed; collective research took precedence over this man's input.

Soon he seemed interested in defining me and was curious if I had taken in the town's "important river." A mental map was described on this clear winter day, "You can only walk a small part of it. The flow from the Black Vermillion connects to a greater body of water, the man made Tuttle Creek." Like most people in Kansas, I knew the large Manhattan water site and dam, but not this connecting waterway.

It was close to eleven and I was hungry. (Priests begin their day at four or five with routine prayers.) After having a Rueben and cream of tomato soup at the local café, I walked the terrain of the narrow Vermillion for about twenty minutes. There was a "no hunting" sign. Then I spotted a few deer beyond the snow-dusted banks. I was never a hunter; such is left to the keen owning a bow and arrow, or the less keen, owning scoped rifles. Eventually, I found what would interest me—a potential three season fishing site. Sitting on a large flat stone, a pleasant thought came to mind. Would I add tall rubber boots and a reel to my sparse personal possessions? Yes, I could see myself perched on a nearby bank. Thoughts of my childhood tickled my ribs.

Driving back on the main highway, an unexpected disappointment rushed through me. It was odd and yet it was not. I was being assigned to another rural town and could not imagine great challenges—the sort one experiences in the inner city or even alternatives like university student ministry. (Manhattan would have been a great assignment!) One consoling fact: the bishop was allowing me to continue my involvement in the Extension Volunteer Program (EVP) of the archdiocese, which I began after the primary changes of Vatican II.

The organization gave parish priests (and recently, nuns) more connections to lay workers—a group I sorely needed. This well-run EVP steered couples and singles to identify their particular talents and find ways to contribute to church and community. There had been some discouragements. A close friend got overly involved and left his priest vows to marry one of the volunteers. Took me weeks to get over that. But later, I would be more disturbed with another priest; he had taken my previous assignment and years later he would discard his vocation to marry the frustrated nun that had shared my coffee with a kiss.

Kind of strange, but one night I dreamt about that nun. The dream was distinctly vivid. A small boy opens the door and catches our intimacy, and then runs back to the school and vomits in the restroom. He holds his secret until the last bell rings. Before leaving the classroom, he writes on the chalkboard, "Sister loves Father!" Next there is an angry man stomping through my office with a letter of disapproval. He is threatening but I simply rise from the desk and hit him in the nose. That was the end. I woke sweating from my inner garment out. My last image held a distinct face—the beautiful wife.

12

Less than two months at my new assignment, I began receiving letters. People of the past missed me, which implied a significant relationship had been severed. Nearly seven years of courtship and I had left the "bride-to-be" at the altar to find another. In the future, there would be another and another. I sat thinking about this destiny: never to marry, go from assignment to assignment, to fall in love with "the next bride," and then leave again. More people. More letters. My eyes started to burn.

Soon I took myself back to the eye specialist only to hear his words, "I'm switching you to glasses—seems you have an allergy to your wetting solution." I was relieved. Cutting the afternoon short, I swung by the post office and found a letter from Ann.

The sixteen-year-old writes, "Dear Father Jake— you have always guided me. I don't know why I'm sad, but I think it's related to the adjustment to a new high school. We must take a bus seven miles because of district education consolidations. There are after school activities, but I'm not allowed to use the car. Our class has fifty students. My best friends have different coursework so we rarely see each other.

Most boys here are so immature. All they think about is sports and short-skirted cheerleaders. But there are more important things—like debate and journalism. My dad does not understand me. My mother is busy with the younger ones. I do a lot of the cleaning and picking up, but when I did more than my share, she allowed me to join the Student Council and the Journalism Club. If I stay on the high Honor Roll, Dad may agree to my borrowing the car. I seem to move from school to chores to church with no life in between. I miss you. Do you mind me saying that? I hope not. I have so many memories."

A simple letter and I chuckled and slipped it in my upper desk drawer. Then the next month, Ann wrote again; the letters would carry on for consecutive weeks—I was touched by her recollection of situations: "Do you remember the first real connection, assisting a nine-year-old who had fallen off the school merry-go-round and you found a wound cleaner and bandaged my knee? And remember that time I was dispirited about the May Crowning, and yet you encouraged me to be happy for the girl selected. And that particular day of defense, when my teacher claimed I was "too bossy" after insisting on the rules in a game. And I shall never forget that most uncomfortable afternoon, when I was ill and the nuns thought I was exaggerating and you still called mother for me. But the great moments were our youth hootenannies; us roasting marshmallows over the campfire with you singing like a country star, and I never wanting to go home."

As done before, I folded her words and placed them in the drawer. When the fifth letter arrived, the tone was different. "Dear Father, I have met a boy…" Ann had met him at a basketball event. Teen emotions. She described her overwhelmed state. And the rascal—I actually knew him. He was from a community living east of the Jesuit College and this boy had a terribly negative reputation. Reality was he had impregnated several girls, and it had fallen on me to reference assistance to the families to locate their daughters to a live-in dorm school for birthing arrangements. This boy had to be two years older than *my dear one*. I actually said it. There it was—the affection—it was obvious! She was like a daughter…a daughter I should never beget.

I was pressed to pick up the phone. Instead, I sent a note off: "Come visit if you can." A week later Ann and her mother drove up and stopped by the rectory. It was a delicate situation, but I was left alone with "my Ann" for at least an hour as her mother visited a friend. That interval gave me opportunity to help Ann define her long-term goals, and at the same time, make evident my concern and affection. If a good relationship could be affirmed, would she see beyond "the here and now?" I hoped. I prayed. I listened. And she talked. A few leading questions—convincing questions—guided with love. Through the grace of God, this teenager was steered beyond the danger of the boy. Yet this created a new problem. As Ann continued to correspond, I was obligated to live up to my commitment—that meant writing back. But the strangest thing—after several communications—it all stopped.

Years later, I learned that Ann's father opened the mail and forbade his daughter to write. I'm fairly sure his wife did not reveal our visit and my intervention. The Irish farmer would have been outraged—*his* daughter taken to another parish to see "that indecent priest!" You see, during this time, rumors had spread that the bishop had relocated me due to "inappropriate behavior." (The kiss?) That wasn't all. Some people would spin enough fallacies to brand me a treasonous person—blaming me for the 1968 closing of their parochial school. I think, soon after, "progressive" became a dirty word.

13

I stayed four years in this second rural assignment. It allowed productive fishing along the Black Vermillion, along with my moderate sermons, regular confessions, predictable baptisms, pompous first communions, glorious confirmations, white weddings and sparse funerals. Since the major tension and upheaval of Vatican II had rested with my last assignment, this parish seemed like smooth sailing. Experience was carrying me along. Then the bishop saw fit to move me again. He had been impressed with my juggling the EVP, and perhaps—though never said—my management of this larger parish without any weird gossip.

It was an incredible day when the prestigious Washburn Campus Minister appointment officially arrived. I called home and shared my enthusiasm. I gloated with a few friends who were kind enough to express congratulations. Next, I went through the required ritual—the announcement from the pulpit. I made a concrete effort to temper joy and appear conflicted. There were no tears in the pews. Maybe I hadn't connected like I had assumed. A mental review: Stable community. Minimal dissension. Less passion. In serving this parish I had been very careful.

Perhaps too cautious. Perhaps built in defenses from the problems with my previous parish had created psychological and physical barriers. I could almost hear the voice of my old mentor in St. Louis. *Enter into their lives.* Had I been really present? If I was building walls this early in my vocation, then I better knock them down.

Breaking walls. The college campus would do just that. Eighteen to twenty-one-year olds read right through adults. Barely into the fifth month working with the university Newman Club, I was required to accompany a dozen Catholic Washburn students on a mid-semester holiday weekend retreat to an historic flat plains cathedral just outside of Hays, Kansas. There were students participants from all over Kansas. The theme was "The Original You." The goal was to assist youth examination of societal peer pressure and how to remain authentic in exploring life values. No tricks allowed. As usual, I fell back on what worked well—attentive listening. Instead of multiple presentations, we would break into small groups for analysis, have team representatives provide their conclusions, and then stage a debate on preferred issues. I would offer no final words except, "Good job, so let's go into meditation and end with prayer."

There were approximately seventy students when we took the final count with Fort Hays State College, Emporia State, Kansas State University, and our Washburn campus students. It is snowing moderately when the retreat begins—and Ann is there. And it is noticeable: my dear one is "grown up." She is wearing a practical wool sweater and proper winter slacks. She is lovely: hair cut shoulder length, no lipstick, and wearing contacts—perhaps prettier than her mother. She tells me she is a seeking a health related or social work degree, planning to work for a program in the Appalachia area. We hug and briefly catch up in the midst of the tight weekend scheduling.

At night, the students were allowed to unroll their backpacks in the lower basement community area. It seemed a bit strange to have co-eds spreading "pillows and beds" within a yard of one another after our session on "life values." I had assumed each group would take separate sides of the vast community space. Nope. These were college students. Lights went out with only one hall lit for restroom location. I tried to make myself comfortable in a near corner, not far from the exit, still thinking someone should be supervising—but supervising what?

I must have been sleeping light. I heard whistling wind turn to howls of a harsh western blast as a huge snowstorm was blowing in—a good twelve inches with three-foot drifting and more accumulation expected. We had listened to the weather reports, and earlier it had crossed my mind that the students and the retreat team might have some delays in getting back to our university settings.

In the late morning Ann sought me out. "I can't stay another night. I know somebody who can help me out." I connected her to a phone. When the fellow picked her up, gut instinct said, here was "her special guy." What person would take a detour off of Highway 36 to collect a young woman in a storm like this? Someone very serious into a relationship.

This wasn't a boy; he was a man—looked ten to fifteen years older than Ann, had dark wavy hair and a smile that opened to even front teeth. He was lean and tall and relieved her backpack the second he neared her side. She would introduce us, but I gathered little data as he quickly escorted her out of the building. Were they lovers? It was the seventies. Lots of lovers. College students could get entangled into all sorts of relationships that spell disaster, often spiraling into depression and poor grades, and yet that reality was almost considered a campus norm. This population was especially challenging from a confessional and counseling perspective, but not an image I could endure if associated to Ann and a possible lover.

She called me in the spring and announced she was engaged. Twenty-going-on-twenty-one—too young. "Are you sure about this?" I asked. Wrong question. I was no longer talking to a sixteen-year-old. "Yes, I am," borderline curt. "Okay, Ann—I believe you. Have you set a date?" I must have sounded parental. "Next year," same voice, still curt. Was she upset I had not congratulated her? For some reason I couldn't, and yet she promised to keep in touch.

When I put down the phone's receiver, I wondered how badly I had "flubbed up." My doubts would nettle me. What was wrong? Didn't Ann say she was going to work with the poor in the Appalachia? I was still worried. What if she got pregnant? Could she follow her goal? I pondered more. Times were modern. With birth control, getting married didn't subjugate young women to male submission and endless babies. Even single Catholic women used the pill, the diaphragm, or other methods. I hated the images sweeping through me: Ann and her fiancé.

For several days I was not myself. I would wake up an hour before my regular time. The first thought always: Would he be good to her? She deserves the best. She is sweet, caring, affectionate and virtuous. I didn't feel hungry. I lost some weight. The shrinking muscles proposed an answer. More biking, more walking. No luck. The nettling didn't cease; it literally turned into a nasty case of ribcage shingles. Linear red blisters. Real burning. Weeks of pain. Endurance required. What was the stressor? It became obvious. Part of me wanted Ann to follow her original desire: to become a nun.

Unknown to me, Ann was struggling. She had hoped to marry a Catholic. Her fiancé would not convert. He didn't like the church requirements. Was this a message from God? She didn't think so. She prayed. There were premarital classes and they received an exemption from the diocese while modifying some qualifying paperwork. Going well. Then not. Original plans for the "Wedding Mass" had been erased; an interdenominational fifteen-minute chapel ceremony would have to substitute—though approved for dual officiates, a priest and a protestant minister. She was resigned. Spending time together had added tension. Her fiancé was pressuring her. The date was adjusted. Small ceremony—few invited. Compromise. Family and close friends. My invitation never came.

Later she told me her mother asked for sensitivity to her father's feelings. That inferred a lot. Under the circumstances, my presence could not be considered, and that negated any possibility of co-officiating the ceremony. I drank three Buds the night of her wedding, and watched TV basketball, then got sucked into an Alfred Hitchcock movie. About midnight, a crazy student called me crying her heart out because her wild younger boyfriend had left her. Quivering sounds of silence and sobs—all heard before. I wanted to slam down the receiver. Instead I listened and listened and then hung up softly and turned out the light. Pulling the blanket over my stressed head and achy chest, I decided to be truly happy for Ann. And my heart was saying, "Dear one—please keep in touch."

14

Awareness

It was 1975. I had been with the Washburn students for eight semesters. Publically branded the *innovative* Father Jake; this represented fearless freedom. Now I had my own schedule and managed numerous retreats. Midway into this position, and my older cousin moved into the private quarters on the campus site. She was close to fifty and had agreed to be my housekeeper and assistant. This was working well as it discouraged the young people from abusing my space, and she could keep an eye on things when I chose to leave town.

There were numerous occasions when her fine frowns hinted students were demanding too much; we would figure out cues that could interrupt conferences or protect me from draining situations. Some decision-making felt interrupted and there were days that seemed "naggy" and yet all right—a simple reminder why I never left the priesthood for married life. And more and more I understood myself. I was a man who craved quiet at the end of the day. Any image of crawling into bed with another felt like a sacrifice, not a comfort. General affection was satisfied by a generation who hugged regularly. The young loved consolation. Such was the poverty of spirit.

Now if the reader compares my situation to Pope Pius XII and his German housekeeper, they are mistaken. Though my cousin was stiff and stoic, she was also practical and generous. Having had several children and grandchildren, she always arranged enough time with them; in addition she took personal vacations. Her state in life brought me a unique perspective. She had lost her husband in an accident and never sought the possibility of another marriage. The single life worked well for her; so we were of like minds and a natural rhythm slowly evolved. One evening per week, we would share private time together. I preferred strumming music and she preferred creating gifts.

"There's a letter." A scented pale green envelope with no return address had caught the attention of my cousin. I sat on my brown leather couch with my guitar still warm after a snappy tune practice for the upcoming outdoor student Mass. She handed me the letter and then sat in the cotton-cushioned chair across the room. Picking up her knitting needles, she bent her head as not to invade, but I found myself reading out loud: "Dear Father Jake, I will be leaving for India next week. Finished my advanced degree in social work. Mitch finished his physician residency and we are contracted for work in Ahmedabad, extending down the west coast, all the way to Goa. We're very excited with the medical mission. Our one-year-old will adapt. Of course, I never made it to the Appalachians but this venture should be interesting. For health care workers—family needs are everywhere. Some updates—one brother is now married and another engaged and that leaves only two undecided, so Mom will have to pray harder if she is going to get a priest. One of my sisters has started college—I'm really proud of her. The other siblings are heavily involved in farm chores and such. Dad owns over a thousand acres—he calls himself 'the biggest farmer on this side of the Kansas River.' Mother is expecting grandchildren any day as my brother's wife is due to have twins. I hope you are well and enjoying your ministry. The students are lucky to have you. There are times I visualize you singing and strumming and praying for all of the needy souls. But don't forget the not so needy—we are blessed but life looks to have rough moments. Still, I think this mission experience will be good for us."

I stopped a moment to look up. My cousin remarked, "That was nice." Nodding, I would agree. She sensed the next lines were not for her ears and rose to get a snack. After she disappeared, a silent read: "I anticipate Mitch will be travelling significantly. I may have to deal with some separation but never aloneness in India! Growing up in a large family should support the adjustment." I leaned back to remember Ann's parents and the numerous times she had oversight of the younger ones. My three siblings to her eleven—more complicated; it must have been crazy.

I returned to the page. It continued, "I'm sorry I have not written for so long. There are unpredictable moments when I hear a particular song or remember a joke or sit in a front pew and your presence feels near. I can even get perturbed when I remember the onerousness—misleading us school kids with *"your"* Saint Patrick's celebration day, the day of your ordination—people will forever be confused if you are Irish. Bohemian German, you later said. Someday, I shall explore your ancestry to prove you have a great-great-great-grandfather who once lived in Ireland! I do pray this finds you and your cousin in good health. Sending my love—Ann."

I read the last four words again; it was 10:00 pm, and my shoulders felt heavy. This young woman was tied to me. Since childhood—intertwined in memories. I was slowly recalling dates in my head. Go backwards. Came to the parish in 1960. She was nine. So born in '51—what month—I couldn't remember. No wait. Spring? That's it. Connected to the May crowning—that tearful occasion for not receiving the appointment to place a wreath upon Mother Mary, her birthday wish that never came to be. In my vocation, there are so many people and occasions to keep straight, but I shall never excuse myself when it concerns her—my dear one. She's twenty-four years old now. At her age I had been in the seminary trying to sort out my future.

15

Mitch and Ann's service dedication would run a long course. In 1979, I moved from campus ministry (with my assistant/housekeeper cousin) back to city parish work, and just as Ann predicted—she had many periods separated from her husband. Now with two children, the parental responsibilities were burdensome. "I often feel like the only parent," she would write, and I would read and nod and absorb her words. Presently into their second furlough, she and her young children were in the United States for a short period—comments revealed missing her siblings and her friends. We arranged to get together.

She looked too thin; had her hair pulled up in a sophisticated style and was wearing a blue-brushed denim suit with a peach colored blouse that brought out the warm tones in her complexion. I noted her poise, but quietly hoped she would put on some pounds and take time for herself. She talked and smiled easily. I was mesmerized by her reflections on ministry and marriage. We spent nearly a full hour discussing the complexities of single verses married mission life.

These reflections were important. I always learned from couples. My ex-priest friends—friends that had taken life partners—often dealt with guilt, or used defensive rationales for broken priestly vows, while *faithfully* married people like Ann carried less baggage; that contrast and that deduction seemed reinforced by the bestselling book called <u>The Thorn Birds</u> by C. McCullough. The writing was excellent, but it included at least six of the seven deadly sins.

I was inquisitive of Ann's feedback. She seemed perturbed when I referred to the novel. Almost vehemently she stated, "I disliked Meggie." The book's setting was Australia, a long epic with complex threads. The main character had a childhood resemblance to Ann in that she had developed a close relationship with a priest. Other than this, nothing resembled our lives. The primary characters had carried feelings too far and had entered into a sexual relationship with far reaching consequences.

"Jake, why did you like that book?" Now she calls me Jake—something closer friends are comfortable with. And I respond limitedly, "I'm intrigued by its popularity. It is said a movie will be made." She tipped her head sideways—an infrequent gesture from youth—and she pressed her lower lip. "Jake, the novel presents women as weak-willed, manipulative, emotionally inconsistent, envious, vengeful." I didn't expect this reaction. "Ann, maybe it's popular because it's sympathetic to the weaknesses of human nature." Part of me was relating to my ex-priest friends who had acted upon their sexual tensions. But Ann was not holding back. "Well, it may sound harsh, but I feel there is no excuse for breaking one's vows." Maybe judgmental, but it offered tremendous assurance that Ann intended to keep her marriage authentic and pure. That re-enforced something important to me: In our close friendship, we had nothing to worry about.

At my regular religious group gathering, I repeated the conversation. One of the priests challenged me. "Jake, are you sure you were not deliberately testing Ann?" My ego was a bit ruffled. "I don't think so." Several looked at one another. Finally the first said, "Let's put it this way—what would you be feeling if Ann had said she could identify with Meggie, that her husband wasn't treating her right, that she could see herself falling in love with a priest—especially if the conditions promoted it?"

Now they had me. *I had over polished my ego.* Perhaps in the course of past campus work, I had convinced myself that young women flocked to me because—well—because they had some basic needs not satisfied by their significant other. And Ann? Had I tried to equate her with these troubled young people? I felt ashamed.

Later into Ann's furlough, Mitch would join her; so the next time we met, the two were side-by-side in my parish office. Their young children were staying with "grandma." Ann pulled out a pocket size photo. It was one of those great poses of three generations. She identified the granddaughters, and the once so beautiful woman, now dimming with age. "I'll bring them next time," referring only to the girls.   Ann would go on to say her goal was to visit every parish I served or would ever serve. It was a sweet compliment. Once again, she was creating memories—or planning memories—memories to share—whatever the circumstances may lead ahead.

The afternoon proceeded with my two guests introduced to the parish team. With Ann distracted by staff members, I was allowed time to get acquainted with Mitch. He seemed an interesting one-on-one conversationalist and an obvious Democrat with very broad worldviews. A mirror of me with the exceptions he was handsome and tall. I was pleased we had *enough* in common. Though to Ann's detriment, Mitch also liked independence—and years later I would learn how dejected and rejected this would make her feel. But this was now, and I concentrated on Mitch and his unassuming words, and I was impressed.

16

After their long period of work in India, Ann and Mitch re-established themselves in the Kansas City area. For years, Ann and I talked on the phone at regular intervals and I kept up with the news. Her last pregnancy would be traumatic—she nearly ended up in the hospital with threatening complications. Post-baby, she went into depression. With my experiences around families, her symptoms were recognizable. I strongly encouraged her to get more support. She would not take the easier route of medication, but she called her mother and rearranged her priorities. I came up to see how she was doing.

At this point in our lives, I am fifty-eight and she is thirty-seven. She tells me Mitch is at a five-day conference. The older kids are in school and the baby is napping. I see a bewildering hurt. In the midst of her emotional pain I am drawn to her like a man to a woman. What is it that makes us men attracted to the vulnerable? She has on a flowing mid-calf skirt and a white loose top that could have been matronly on another woman—on her, its youthful and perfect. Her clean shiny hair is partially bereted to the left, emphasizing a flawless complexion. She and I finish our apple tart and are taking a second cup of coffee—

mine strong, hers decaffeinated.

"Jake, this has really gotten me down—hormones can do weird things." I knew she was making an assessment of postpartum depression, but I was thinking of something else. "Ann, is there more to it?" She looked up with such sad beautiful eyes that I got prepared to soak up a threatening fountain. "I guess there is." Soon her buried conflict: Mitch had never wanted children, and yet Ann had strongly felt marriage should include parenthood. Furthermore, it appeared Mitch had been extremely perturbed about this third pregnancy. Even Ann had been caught off guard. She had been taking coursework as to advance her professional flexibility. And then, "it just happened."

"We love our son," this is said with no sweetness. The baby is stirring in the background. Should I prepare to leave? It felt cowardly. But I had a sudden weakness. Now I knew enough to make me angry with this husband who wanted no children. I could not be objective, and what I was about to say, was partially selfish. But I would say it. "Ann, if you were misled—now ask yourself—is this a valid marriage?" I would briefly clarify the Catholic Church's conditions pertaining to annulment and the length of its process, and would conclude by saying, "I want you to call me *for anything,* or any reason." Her eyes look desolate. No further emotion. This is part of depression. She is so overwhelmed by her aloneness—and stupid me had just added to her burden. I should have waited. Her baby is stirring again and the moment passes.

When we head toward the door, I turn to hug her—she feels limp. I reach upward. I stroke her soft hair—ever so gently—so mindful she might collapse. Stepping apart, "Are you going to be okay?" She manages a feigned smile. "For today?" I check again. She nods. I walk down the steps, enter my car, start the engine; I look toward the house, and she waves me on.

17

It was over a month before I would hear from her again. The letter was almost formal. Referencing the five-day conference, Ann described Mitch's return with an armful of roses and a surprising gift. "He is so kind and attentive...the new diamond is next to my gold band"; and then she described a man who supported her going back to a career ladder, after their youngest was weaned. She wrote, "I plan to find an older sitter; one who will come to the house ensuring the children's present program. Mitch is a hundred percent in agreement." My thought—*he had an affair.* My chest was tight. I folded the letter too quickly and placed it under the thick correspondence in my drawer. I breathed in, I exhaled: *"Dear Ann—be attentive."*

My city parish was in a tight neighborhood and it posed a good challenge. The bishop had projected we would outgrow our building and so the diocese was into the construction of another church near Overland Park—prime property had been donated. It was perfect timing. I needed distraction. So for eighteen months I was wrapped up into this incredible project. I have a brother who is an architect and his volunteered consultant services saved the diocese a hundred thousand dollars. This came with the non-written condition I would be appointed to the new parish. While overseeing elements of this evolving situation, I continued to serve the older church community from my small residence directly across the street.

During this phase, Ann stopped in after attending a licensure mandated continuing education course. She was wearing a short split skirt—a bit flashy but practical as she could ride any transport. I provoked her lightly, "I sense an approaching mid-life rebellion." She answered, "Yeah—I could be classified as a non-traditional student." I showed her my repaired motorcycle, saying, "This is how I get about between here and the construction project..." My cousin, who was still my housekeeper, would offer refreshments—she knew my guest well. We answered affirmative, but I hinted I'd take Ann for a spin afterwards. My cousin frowned.

We scooted through the streets and walked the site and scooted back to my residence. After Ann left, my cousin reprimanded me harshly. "She is a mother with three children—what if you had been in an accident—how would you explain that to the bishop!" She had a good point. I was so pleased to see Ann that I had acted impulsively. My cousin continued, "I was going to invite her for your birthday, and now I'm not sure." How this was relevant to the impulse, I don't know, but certainly she reminded me that I was not in any position for such foolishness. However, I felt proud about the building project and did not regret that Ann had seen the process.

Church of the Holy Spirit. Not only would we have a large modern structure, we were promised a huge community space. Still I pushed for an unusual addition and won approval for an adjacent chapel to commemorate our "sister church" in San Salvador, capital of El Salvador. My old congregation had conducted several trips to Central America and sponsored mission groups to assist an impoverished Catholic community. These were dangerous situations—the country was in the middle of a civil war—which had gotten worse by the negative influence of the United States. The added chapel was our small act of reparation.

Civil war mixed with political and religious elements is always horrific. Before he was assassinated nearly a decade ago, Bishop Romero had been among the El Salvadorians fighting for social justice. This had included unionized rights, agrarian reform, better wages, access to health care, and freedom of expression. As a social activist, Bishop Romero had been a voice for the voiceless. His documented quote, "There are many things that only can be seen through the eyes that have cried," was probably referencing crimes against women. In El Salvador, when a woman has a miscarriage, it is automatically assumed she has attempted abortion, and thus faces a long-term prison sentence.

More of his words moved me—words sounding

similar to the Vincentian philosophy of go and serve: "A church that does *not provoke* any crisis, preach a gospel that does *not* unsettle, proclaim a word of God that does *not* get under anyone's skin, or a word of God that *does not* touch the real sin of society in which it is being proclaimed. What kind of Gospel is that?" Bishop Romero's words would stir my soul; if I could ever claim an ounce of what this man did for the poor I should face my God with more courage.

To minister in San Salvador—though very limitedly—required a modified passport and ordinary street attire because Catholic clergy were often profiled. During my two trips, I had to move about like a common tourist—any white collar would have incited suspicion with possible arrest. I'm not sure my bishop would have approved of this approach, but he had limited experience to what was necessary to blend in with the lay volunteer group. All was kept quiet. My traveling group enabled me to do what I had to in order to keep safe. One woman in the group was especially good at the façade. She would walk the San Salvadorian streets holding my elbow as if we were best friends.

Some might say I should not have been in this country under such circumstances, but I felt it was important to *see the needs of the people first hand*. This effort *was not the deepest root* in the lives of the poor, but I felt it was a way for me to contribute. As multiple trips allowed, our committed group organized a local San Salvadorian church community and set up means to filter in financial assistance and aid. The process was risky and yet the endeavor was too important to abandon. This led to our official adoption of the "sister church."

18

It was spring. Ann loved the chapel. She and Mitch and the three children had come down to visit the nearly finished project. With their past experience in India, their questions were interesting and I enjoyed the lengthy exchange. This was the second time around Ann's husband—though knowing their personal marital background and having dealt with my own "run-away feelings," this did not prevent me from attempting to understand the man. I think he sensed my closeness to his wife and yet seemed comfortable with our relationship. That made the guy more likable.

I've had run-ins with jealous husbands, so it's refreshing to be around men who don't feel threatened. Modern priests are vulnerable; we mix more with people and it brings complexities. Added to that, Vatican II allowed us face-to-face confessions—with no obligation of a dividing screen. Confessions could morph from thirty-second starters to short or longer discussions, and even future consultations. This has some pitfalls in terms of time management, but also in terms of boundaries. A person could be at the rectory or church longer than anticipated and gossip could follow. And if a wife took too long—that risked a mouthful from an irate husband. With Mitch's background, I was fairly sure he had no concerns. In his protestant denomination, ministers had counseled in the face-to-face format for hundreds of years. And with consideration to Mitch's medical career, he probably faced situations more complex than mine.

But after Ann and her family took off and headed back to the Missouri side of Kansas City, I meditated in the small chapel. She was my dear one. I had basic knowledge of her marriage, children, in-laws, siblings, her mom, her dad, her work, and passion about social issues—especially the poor and the elderly and the need for universal health care. For years she had been part of multiple projects that addressed external problems—but when it came to internal conflicts, she had not cracked her shield since my untimely mention of "qualifications for annulment." It was that sensitive stretch after the birth of her son, and I regretted my impulse to offer her a way out.

Through the summer Ann would pick up the phone for a thoughtful chat. She was very respectful of my time and commitments, and I didn't want to diminish the importance of shared "history." We had invested in each other. Our lives would soon take a new depth. We spoke of starting a tradition; maybe there was concern we would drift apart. Ann came up with the idea: no matter how busy, we should always connect in May and October, our birthday months. My birthday was the first around the bend and I had arranged to meet at Perkins—this probably reflected my age! She agreed to the location and correlated the chosen hour to compliment her free time after an educational class.

The original intent was late afternoon for coffee and dessert. Twenty minutes before the set hour, there was an interruption and I was called out—a crisis—a parishioner was threatening suicide. Ann got my message and said she would go over to the rectory and wait for me. My cousin was there, so no problem.

They must have exchanged two hours well; when I walked in, they were chattering away like old friends. It was a bit unnerving; and I felt famished. Ann and I took off immediately, and she chose a convenient place I'd never been before—a cozy corner "ma and pa" establishment. After stuffing myself and watching Ann nibble over a light salad and drink her basil tomato soup from a cup, she proposed we take an autumn stroll in the nearby park. It proved a tempting setting to vent the frustrations and irritabilities of unpredictable demands in my parish work. Within several strides, I was the penitent and she the priest.

While confessing my sins of impatience, anger and reactivity, she took my arm and we kept walking. It was getting dark, and I knew we best return and yet spontaneously I leaned over and kissed my dear companion. She pulled back, very quickly. "What was that?" she reproved, but I only laughed. "Ann, it's just a kiss." (This was the same man who had judged the rebellious nun.) She shook her head and then said something throwing me off, "Jake, be careful;

sometimes a kiss is more intimate than intercourse." I apologized. We walked back—silently—to our cars. It felt tense, and then it didn't after she gave me a brief hug, and took off. But had she forgiven me?

19

December rolled around and Ann's 1989 Christmas correspondence arrived as a form letter, processed for a hundred friends and family members with a small personal note near the lower border. If this was a subtle cue her life was getting busier and she was retracting, I got the hint.

In spite of my overwhelming seasonal liturgical demands, my handwritten letter spilled, "My dear one, the last time we were together, you allowed me to vent." I didn't refer to my physical gesture; for me, it had been "pure" affection; and since I had buried Ann's intimacy remark, the opportunity to analyze it had been erased. But in wanting a return to confidence and freedom, I shared a situation bothering me. "I have another opportunity to go to El Salvador and one of my staff has decided to take the trip. She is a fantastic person, but has been through a lot. In the office setting, I often delegate and she accomplishes a great deal as long as there is continuous encouragement. The hard part—she consumes more and more of my attention."

Ann wrote back, "I surely empathize. I have similar challenges with my staff—some cling to me and will hardly venture alone, though I believe them quite capable of more. It is hard to be firm, but I remind them there's only one of me, and I'm not able to spread myself like butter over multiple loaves." I smiled to myself—I surely identified. Yes, her comment held solid footing. She would offer: "Sometimes we give away a loaf, and all survive." She ended with, "Jake, by your loving and attentive nature, you make the person you are listening to, or relating to, feel exceptional, like cinnamon bread! It's a gift and a curse. This person you speak of wants to stay close to you. With prayer, she will eventually wean away—and toward a new path! As for travelling with her to El Salvador—I think you know the answer."

Ann was right. My focused attention on people brought me a lot of followers; and this created workers for the Lord—and it bore handicaps. But change and new approaches are necessary. I disliked making enemies. Once I had a past co-worker who swore to bring the bishop's wrath upon me; he had balked at my intermittent outdoor Masses for the homeless. (I used to do them for the college students also.) In another situation, an older parish member accused me of excess ministry with shut-in communion distribution; in his thinking I wasn't prioritizing. And recently, a new councilman had cited my bending the rules for liturgical music; he said the young were allowed secular choices in instrumental adaptations. My "unsettling" or "getting under the skin" had provoked crises—just like the late martyr Romero had described. But I just wasn't up for assassination—not even *character assassination!*

These thoughts guided my final decision: I decided not to go to El Salvador, but my staff person went along with the group. While she was gone, I oriented another person to potentially take over her position. Then I arranged an interview for a prestigious "assistant director situation" in another parish, betting my staff person would go for it. Everything seemed to work out. My cousin expressed her opinion. "I always thought that woman was potential trouble." At first, I didn't agree with this deduction. In many ways I had admired the courage of this person, who had endured an awful divorce from an extremely abusive husband, and actually, I missed our day-to-day interaction. Even so, my cousin rattled off incidents on the digits of both hands with potential for detrimental consequences. OK—now I admitted fires could be lit.

Days passed. The various incidents my cousin had referred to were unnerving me. Soon I was evaluating multiple ministries. More incidents would pop up. Most were related to the college ministry. Some of the young had been unstable, like the distraught young woman sitting face-to-face, who had seemed out of control; during a long intervention I had leaned over to grasp her jean covered knees; it had been a gesture to assure someone cared, and also cue her to gain control. And then there was the male student who had stalked me, until I called the bishop; the advice he gave could have created a negligence report. The worst incident, related to the student who committed suicide after our Catholic Newman Club group had drunk excessively, following the campus "Jesus Christ Superstar" production.

Then on the harmless side, I had good friends: several fishing buddies—one was a nun. Several times we stayed out late and returned to the rectory to fry fresh catch—imagine the misinterpretations. Where most acquaintances intermittently emitted troubles or heavy woes, my fishing buddies had refreshing personas—they brought balance and rest to my tiring ministry.

20

Conscience

Into a new decade. Maybe it was the drizzle that stopped; I could have guessed the timing unusual. Ann's oldest daughter was in high school. The middle child was in grade school, and the youngest in a daycare play program Ann was approaching her 39th birthday and we had bumped up our plans. Mitch was at a medical conference, and in her comfortable way she had invited me to their home place. The sprawling ground level was remodeled; its earth tones emphasized. New marvelous large windows allowed natural light. The back patio opened to an early mix of perennials attracting butterflies and birds and anyone to stay...

Ann knows I like Bud—not the light—a real six percent. While out on the patio taking in the rainbow, she announces, "I have some news." Ann still looks ageless. Another baby? Though these late surprises for career women were happening more often these days, I say nothing. I wait. *No baby.* Instead, she says, "Mitch wants to become a Catholic." My response sounds odd—even to myself. "What brought this on?" She shifts in the chair to reach for her own beer.

Without looking at me she says, "You remember from my last note, his parents died weeks apart—his mother in March and father soon after. He was close to them; they were in their mid-eighties and went quickly. His thinking was to convert after their deaths; I guess it would have been upsetting for them." I note, "Still feels sudden, or does it?" Our lounge chairs are situated adjacent to one another, so I can't read her eyes and actually that doesn't matter with her sunglasses. She continues as if my interruption was premature. "He had no problem with the children being raised Catholic, so I truly believed he would—someday." Now she stops. I chug down some Bud. "And Ann, you are happy?" Nothing for a hanging moment as if her silence was saying, "I should be happier." I wait again.

Then she explains, "He has been carrying something for a long time—says he's been unfaithful—now has it in his head, he'll be cleansed with Catholic confession, and we'll have a new beginning." I was listening intently as she gets to the depth of the matter. "I think I'm angry—he makes it all sound so easy and infers this is what confession is all about—just pronounce your sin and start all over."

And now I would ask, "How long ago was this?" She removes the sunglasses and wipes them off with the edge of her light spring sweater, explaining, "Right after the birth of our last one—while I was in the middle of my depression." Then I was thinking, *Dear God—I guessed right.* Reaching my hand out, she takes it; we're both looking straight ahead. "Jake, how

does a man keep that to himself, for so many years?"
I knew the answer. "A man will avoid guilt as long as
possible."

A week later, I was feeling under the weather. I
caught a bad cold—really rare for me, but it was nasty
enough to make me slow down and reflect on what
had bothered me since my afternoon with Ann. *Her
husband wants to become Catholic—why was she
dwelling on the negative?* Basically Mitch is a good
man. Why can't I be harsher? I don't know the full
story. I've never heard his side. Ann is no angel. She
can be quite assertive. Sometimes, she has tough
expectations—maybe too high. Now I imagine her
whining, or yelling at her children, or at her husband,
or manipulating, or anything that makes her look as
common as Mitch. There it lay bold: Men defending
men. Where was my empathy for Ann? My dear one is
emotionally recuperating from a torrid past and I've
not said a prayer.

I would not be given information of Mitch's choice for
a confessor, but Ann's husband would offer I administer
the other sacraments. All culminated at the end of the
summer. A large Mass was performed with the bishop
approving communion and confirmation during the
same service. It was quite moving. I had done such for
numerous couples in my ministry but this ceremony
lifted me to another height. I felt an overwhelming love
for Ann as I prayed for her eternal happiness. If she
was able to forgive Mitch and his sins of the past—truly
forgive—she should reach a high level of spirituality.

21

Normally, I am a very positive person. I encourage harmless humor and gentle teasing. I like coining new words and creating metaphors. One of my friends reminds me that I had called the young in the late sixties, "the termites." Guess I saw them eating away the old ideas as to make way for new. We had a good laugh. I know how to rest. I am a man who enjoys life, be it playing a guitar, casting a fish line, sailing a boat, riding a motorcycle, skiing the slopes, and most recently, communicating via ham radio and planning for early retirement. Looking from the outside in, it's a good life—a life that hardly imitates a discipline of traditional priesthood and strict attitudes of poverty.

But I know—with God's help—I have influenced people to see their faith as relevant; I have inspired deeper spirituality via the Vatican II changes; I have walked with San Salvador's inner-city poor; I have marched politically for broad social justice; I have strongly supported equality between men and women; I have sought fair treatment for our religious sisters. And I still seek sexism corrections in our worship music and communication. Maybe I have a habit of provoking crises...

My peers told me that the bishop had been tolerant

of my independent ways, and in 1993, my luck ran out when a new conservative appointee was made to the diocese. I was sixty-three, and that meant seven more years of church service before an official stipend retirement. A great ministry shortage continued—and now priests were being externally recruited. What irony. For centuries, North America had sent priests abroad and now we were bringing others to minister to us; and at the same time, our immigrant population was increasing, and so w*e needed* clergy who spoke multiple languages—having "foreign priests" looked like a blessing to me.

Getting older and less flexible to parish movement, I hoped to stay with the Church of the Holy Spirit—somewhat selfish to be serving a church population located in the "upper crust" neighborhood of Kansas City, Kansas, but these people were extremely generous with time and money and I was very impressed by the continued outreach to the inner city needs, as well as their strong "sister" support to the very poor people in Central America; this certainly was not saving the world but it was leaving a defined footprint.

Mitch and Ann seemed occupied with juggling careers and home life. Where did the time disappear? Their oldest daughter was in college, and the other daughter and the young son had a ways to go. I was at a retreat one weekend, and later in a shopping mall looking for small treats for my great nieces and great nephews. My two brothers and my only sister make sure I participate in specific events. While shuffling from one store to another, two mature lovers were strolling beyond, holding hands with a nimble hip motion brushing one against the other. The back of her hair looked remarkably familiar. The man was wearing a blue Royals cap with the beak turned backwards. Later in the day, I was taking the elevator to my hotel room and whom should I meet? Ann and her husband; he was wearing the blue cap. We exchanged pleasantries and I reminded them it had been a long time since I had heard from them—actually it was a direct reminder to Ann that she had forgotten our birthday promise.

The coming October was corrected. It was my sixty-fifth and my cousin and several others had arranged a surprise "senior" party. (I'm not terribly amused by surprise gatherings.) The group was small enough, but I was smelly and damp from head to toe after a full afternoon of late season fishing. Everyone seemed to enjoy the joke as I excused myself briefly to change from soiled clothing. I probably mumbled the whole time under my breath.

The simple sandwiches and cake and hot cocoa felt like an adolescent regression. Funny, I think this was their intent. Nevertheless, the cards were hilarious and I was pressed to read every word. After the guests left, Ann helped my cousin with cleanup. The weather was turning and looked threatening: possible hail. We checked the news—under a thunderstorm watch. I suggested Ann call home and tell her family she may stay the night. My cousin raised her brows but offered to prepare the spare room. Ann was vacillating back and forth, and then went with my suggestion.

Thunder and more thunder, and out went the lights. Ann told my cousin (who is five years older than me) that she'd finish the cleanup, so my tired and dedicated housekeeper climbed the stairs guided by a flashlight. I lit some candles on the lower level, and then Ann and I sunk into the sofa chairs. If there ever was a moment of eternal youth, this was it. The flames were dancing and shadows playing off the walls. Exterior wall insulation stifled the heavy rain sound. Hail never hit. Storm warnings diminished. We drank hot herbal tea in thick mugs. Ann teased about the birthday cards and we read some over again. She asked for an honest reaction to the surprise party. I made her promise she would never do it again. She laughed, and I imagined "my dear one" never leaving.

We talked about life and what the end of the decade might look like. Then I disclosed—I couldn't resist telling her: a *parish member* had donated land for my future retirement house. It was close to eleven and this perked her up. "Tell me more!" My elaboration: "It's the perfect spot—an earth home on a south slope next to a large lake where I can walk and bike and fish and sail!" She wanted me to describe the floor plan. "Open, wood-burning fireplace, moderate size kitchen with a double sink and a dishwasher, two bedrooms, two baths, laundry, and a walkout patio." It must have sounded large. Ann was taking a slow breath as her eyes twinkled, "Are you sure you didn't leave something out?" I took the defensive—sixty-five-year-olds can be sensitive. "Oh yes, I should say the garage—actually, a shop and a garage." Her grin flashed a near acclimation, and yet being it was late, her voice was low, "My oh my Jake, someone loves you!"

She was partially accurate. Not just one person, but several parish members were close to me. Church of the Holy Spirit was an exceptional assignment. But on this stormy evening, neither Ann nor I knew the precise date I planned to leave *this* bride—my last parish bride. And we couldn't know we'd soon shift to the ugly of ugliest times—though scandals had historically followed the church, new revelations lie ahead. Was I tired of being associated with white collars and black cassocks? I told Ann that I wished to retire as soon as eligible, before things got worse. Sure, I had plenty of energy and the bishop needed me, but he wasn't my favorite guy. He had given me a hard rub about the specifics of my retirement plans. (I planned to put my assets in a trust for Holy Spirit ministry and the church in San Salvador—not directly to the diocese.) Overall, I believed the bishop doubted my vows of poverty and obedience, but thought me too old to investigate the chastity part.

When Ann had gone to the spare room and I faced myself alone—my joy met a cloud heavier than any storm. What if fate had taken us elsewhere? What if I had left the priesthood? What if I had married Ann? I'm only seven years older than her husband... Why did I love her so much? There were no answers—except she represented the perfect friendship—one based on time-tested trust. I had known her thirty-five years and she had never crossed a forbidden line. As for me, I wasn't sure, though my long-ago kiss was considered brief and innocent. Or was it? If Ann had been receptive, would I have allowed more? Was this an admission of guilt on a stormy night? My conscience was weary; it was late and I put all aside.

Ann left very early the next morning. My cousin entered the kitchen looking refreshed, until she saw me washing the dishes. "Ann didn't finish them?" I shook my head slightly, "The lights never came on—we gave up and went to bed." Her eyebrows lifted severely. "You know what I mean," I said. She glared at me. "Hope Ann doesn't get the third degree." I stacked the last plate. "Mitch will understand." She shook her head and left the room. I considered that my cousin had lived with me long enough. Who needs a housekeeper? I didn't mind dishes or dusting or laundry and simple meals.

Within eight weeks, I achieved greater independence. Six months after my cousin left, she passed quietly in the night, dying mercifully. She had been a good soul—now she was with her husband in heaven and probably keeping an eye on me.

22

Sin

Five years since my sixty-fifth birthday and I was still located at Holy Spirit's parish. The priest shortage was getting more critical and scandals continued. The local bishop was talking me into an extension. I was bargaining for a fully paid trip to Canada, and so two years later, on July 27, 2002, among many pilgrims and sponsors for the Youth World Day festival, I counted myself among thousands listening to Pope John Paul II, extremely frail, holding his hands high—though unsteadily—to bestow his blessing after an incredible Holy Mass gathering. People were hushed and quiet—trying to grasp his concluding words. Difficult. I had a copy of his prior sermon in my pocket. The topic was: <u>Sin and the Church</u>.

Before the last leg home, I took out the sermon and studied it. The Catholic Church was in trouble—the pain and burden apparent in every word of the Holy Father. He wrote of the history of reconciliation and healing—pointing at specific countries and specific individuals. He clarified that sin or abuse from a priest is a suicidal act. Stronger points made: The vocational bond to "Christ as the other" (verses human bond to another human) is lost by any deliberate rejection of God through evil acts. Internal balance is destroyed. Contradiction and conflict arise. The emotionally and spiritually injured will close off or isolate from the church. When there is anger and revenge, the temptation of rage exists.

The Holy Father had been emphatic about his "injured people." A summary: *The sin is personal!* And furthermore—by its very act it creates a memory or a "history." Acknowledgment of the sin and/or injury is absolutely necessary; it's the statement of truth. Love, respect, truth. And if falsely accused (pertaining to clergy), one must learn from suffering, and re-examine their actions with a new attitude. *Falsely Accused. Good God, that would be terrible! Everything you stood for would be taken away.* The Pope's teaching dwelt on reconciliation. Always, love must establish justice—which means re-establishing the relationship, and re-integration back in society. Only the warmth of human relationships can overcome sin and bring about necessary healing. My heart agreed with the Pope: One can say that truth and healing of memories ward off future generations of division, because in this sense, every sin is social as well as personal. The Pope had sounded a warning. In the years ahead, this warning would unfold.

Mid-October; the day had finally arrived. The parish was sending me off. The great farewell. The fall weather was crisp and cool and hundreds showed up—this included people and staff from years of service. The indoor Mass was celebrated in the usual progressive style, meaning all references to "man" were changed to "humankind," and all references to Trinity held a balance of masculine and feminine. The music was deliberately selected and modified to reflect inclusiveness. I had been doing this for so long it seemed second nature. If the bishop had been present, I wouldn't have changed it. As the communion line formed, every person known was called by name. "John, the Body of Christ, Jane, the Body of Christ, and so on. Unknown names were few.

During the reception, it was pleasing to hear, "Father, do you recall when..." Yes and no. Who can remember everything over forty-five years of ministry? It was tempting to allow a convincing pretense. I would say, "Not sure, but I want to hear it again!" The person would smile or laugh, and usually I received a good tale. My staff chose the funny stories with only two dramatics squeezed in. Some were a bit teary-eyed. One staff person frowned repetitively. Later, she seemed sort of off to herself. When the event was nearly over, I looked for her to share a few words. "Where's Irene?" I asked. Another staff person stated, "She's left." Frankly I didn't think much about this, until much later, when an accusation was made against me. But on this day, I was quite caught up in loving and leaving and moving to my lakeside home.

23

By 2003, the worst scandals of the church had subsided—or so I thought. But an undercurrent was frightening. Our northeastern church leadership in Kansas had begun a repressive movement, and the bishop on the other side of the state line preached and functioned like Vatican II was responsible for the Church's problems. Seminarian applicants were being filled with candidates who saw greater value in pre-sixties philosophy. I shall clarify they were not extremists like the Pope Pius X Society—a cult-like break off from the Roman Catholic Church. Ironically, that extreme society had taken over the old Jesuit Campus where I had years of good friendships, where retreats had been once popular, where there had been deep discussions and prayerful experiences that instilled in me hope for a better future. Ann had heard about that group and reported a new center built thirty minutes from her residence. Looked as if the Pope Pius X Society had intentions to spread over the Midwest.

I grieved to see everything our generation had worked hard for, now starting to disintegrate. The regressive elements were proclaiming the root cause of the pedophile abuse could be traced to the inaction of Pope John Paul II. Had there been a cover-up? It almost made me come out of my semi-retirement and put a stronger voice forward. After my experience in Canada, I wondered if he was *only* a man of words.

Even though I had removed myself from any parish appointments, I was assisting the diocese with part-time Masses, for priests needing relief, or for those taking a brief sabbatical. I also assisted with liturgical community confessions. I resisted going back to a direct paid parish position, though it was offered. My preference remained working with the Benedictine nuns in Atchison. I claimed my historic connection to this congregation and enjoyed saying services for these lovely spirit-filled women.

Just about this time, Ann informed me that she and Mitch were looking to build a vacation home. I suggested she drive up my way on her birthday—an hour-and-a-half distance to look at some building sights close to the lakeside area. "Turn on the first left, after the turn south, and park your vehicle at the small retreat center—I'll meet you there—oh yes, wear good trail shoes." Semi-retirement had re-energized me; I could probably out walk most thirty-year-olds.

Middle-aged, forever young Ann was wearing slim blue jeans with a tank top and open buttoned outer shirt that could be removed and tied about her waist if she should desire the sun. Her brown hair was caught up and twisted behind her head and reinforced with a thick band. She was rubbing extra sunscreen on the back of her neck before adjusting a chin tied straw hat upon her head. I watched her brief preparation. Typical to her personality, she was thorough. Carefully, but expediently, she applied lip balm and sun lotion and placed her keys in the miniature side pack clipped to her belt.

We both had water bottles, and we took the trail. With this, we had to pass through barbed wire fencing—Ann and I knew exactly how the pros did it, ducking and squeezing through as each took turns stepping on the bottom line and lifting the top wire. It was always little things that endeared her to me. The things we did automatically. I showed her some tree filled lots, and then we neared my earth home. Her eyes widened, "This is it!" I knew she was happy for me. I would show off every nook and cranny, including my welding shop—a place for creating metal art for charity fundraisers. She was interested in the tools and methods and of course that pleased me. Later, we settled into shaded chairs with sun mint tea, and being ice chilled, it tasted delicious.

"Anything to eat?" It would have been great fun to show off—I was pretty good at pan-fried fresh water fish. She declined the full meal, but we ended up putting together a light snack. A glance given to her new cell phone, the popular portable device—hinted of departure, yet she asked about the neighbors. "Six to seven homes down the road—several retired couples, two young families, and add an old bachelor like me, and we're a real community!" She giggled just like a kid of long ago. I wanted to kiss her lightly, but I had learned my lesson. We walked back through the empty high grass lots and passed under barbed wire. I reminded her that she was welcomed to return anytime, and then she left for home.

24

Ann and her husband ended up building a spacious stucco home at the highest point in the county on the Missouri side—totally open with an incredible view—quite a contrast to a secluded wooded site. If home reflects the owners, it pushed me to ask, "Are we now different or was this more about Mitch?" And the next time the question was answered.

She had called and asked a favor, concerning her niece. A February '05 wedding shower, and it was fifteen minutes from my place. Ann said a heavy snow was in the forecast, but she didn't want to miss this occasion. "Could I come to your place the night before—that will put me in navigable distance to the party?" I hesitated, but said, "Sure—of course—my guest room is set up." I would learn later she was angry with her husband.

She arrived with a moderate size bag and parked her all-terrain vehicle in the proper direction; my broad driveway would allow for a smooth exit if the road got too slick. It was close to suppertime. I had thawed some good protein and was able to fix fried fish. She had brought fresh wheat bread, and we added a course of thin soup; there was no better way to top this off than a good cup of Joe and a fired-up wood stove. Ann's posture looked relaxed, but her eyes said something else. Slightly glassy and too serious.

Leaning back with a quilted throw around her shoulders, she hinted that Mitch was going through some sort of weirdness; it had been a long time since Ann had revealed anything intimate. Then it fell out. Drugs—the enhancement kind. Was something wrong with this? She proceeded with her point of view. "So what happened to the natural laws of the church? Women have been lectured against using the artificial, but now it's okay for men." Whoa! We were not talking about birth control; we were talking about improving a married couple's degree of intimacy—where was Ann going with this?

"These darn unnatural drugs could blow out the veins and it will herniate him eventually, and then he'll resort to direct injections, and before he knows it, he'll be rendered sexually dysfunctional." I could see she was really peeved. Her husband was a physician and she thought he should have studied the literature and done more research. Yet I was thinking it was *his body,* and that he would risk anything (though it sounded like a short-term fix) to keep his manhood. More thoughts were piling up too. *Ann's an attractive woman who is and looks significantly younger than her husband—*he probably wants to please her, and maybe he fears not keeping up. Good gracious, women sure do think differently than men!

Ann was still talking. As a priest, I had been involved in direct counseling for years. I had heard every imaginable complaint and disappointment, and listened to the severest cruelty and abuse between spouses. This was the first time I had a discussion on the so-called male-enhancement drugs. Up to now, I had assumed these drugs were assisting in the quality of marriage.

From Ann's point of view, I had it all wrong. They were full of danger: it potentially shortened the sexual lives of couples; it allowed malfunctioning mentally disturbed men to rape women or children; it promoted outside affairs or hotel quickies; it tested loving and natural sexual expression; and in the long viewpoint, it could damage a man's physiology. For years the church has taught the human body "is the temple of the Holy Spirit," and yes, we should treat our physical nature with high respect.

But wait. There was more to Ann's convincing argument. Abruptly, I had an image of black-cloaked men abusing small children—the pedophiles and their defamation of the Catholic Church. Has the hierarchy been so blinded? This was exactly why we needed broader participation in our policy-making, in the critical discussions about human behavior—especially lay input into papal decrees or encyclicals!

It seemed like weeks later and I received a call from Ann thanking me for my hospitality; she reported the February wedding shower had gone nicely. I didn't reveal that our last discussion had exhausted me. Instead I said, "I hope to see you in several months." She replied, "Sounds delightful." Then she apologized for dwelling on "that personal subject"—and again referring to the discussion, "I think I got carried away." But I assured her that I was grateful for her thought-provoking words. She asked about my general plans. I reminded her of the March skiing trip planned for Colorado. "Good for you!" She sounded impressed. I bragged slightly about my "stamina." She laughed. Her last words sounded almost maternal, "Jake—take care."

25

A broken hip is extremely painful. My friends had been a short distance from the slope when the accident occurred. Maybe I wasn't attentive, maybe it was the condition of the snow, or perhaps, my own aging body wasn't as strong as I believed. I ended up in the hospital with major surgery, and then was informed of the lengthy recuperation.

After being in south Kansas City for several weeks with my sister's family, I convinced them my bone could heal at home. The pin inside allowed minimal external bracing, but without full weight bearing, I would need to alternate between cane and walker. Ann had offered to help but pride got in the way of good sense; I insisted everything was coming along "pretty well." I think I hurt her feelings. What are good friends if they cannot help each other? But my ego was getting in the way. I didn't want her to regard me as a crippled old man.

I missed seeing her in May but she wrote a short note. "I've decided to give notice." She had been overseeing the referral department of a major health delivery system. "I'll do volunteer services; it will free me up." Ann's father had died some time back but her mother was ailing and I understood where she was coming from: though she had many siblings, she was the "most qualified" person in her family and feeling responsible. And what she didn't say was just as clear. I had not allowed her to be present in my time of need. *Oh Ann—I'm sorry!* Now, I knew for sure I had deprived her of the loving assistance previously offered.

Men can be pretty stupid. Not only do we find it difficult to read the hearts of women, we have discriminated against them for centuries. I've heard more than once "most men make lousy lovers." Well, we priests can be lousy listeners.

After my hip accident, I had plenty of time to re-examine our heavy discussion on drugs. Male-enhancement. Clever advertising. The TV commercials were ramping up drug popularity as if it was the greatest thing since sports and beer. And all three were connected. I started reading statistics on human trafficking and realized my local city was as guilty as any large metropolitan area. Supposedly, hormonal aggression rises among big selling sport ticket holders with fancy hotels and dark bars. Pimps line up "the products"; teens and preteens are coveted "items." As if these facts weren't shocking enough, a news story broke out about a local priest and bishop involved in online pedophile pornography. Online abuse—a growing national disgrace. Even in these associations—could male enhancement drugs be tied to addictive Internet behavior?

Whether pedophiles, pimping or pornography,

these widespread addictions would have to be solved. Money and greed and sex and abuse... It would take a David to fight a Goliath. The competitive have power. Rich companies have power. If taken to court, how would the injured, the "weaker person," prove them guilty. Just as I was hesitating to become a David, something worse than a broken hip knocked me over.

26

The bishop notified me that *a quiet investigation* was going on. It referenced a serious incident "some time ago." There was a middle-aged woman accusing me of "inappropriate behavior"—whatever that meant—the inference indicated sexual allegations. Having counseled thousands, there were situations when I had hugged a person just as a doctor or nurse might hug a patient. Other times, I had held a hand to assure someone they were not alone in this big bad world. Of course I had special friendships, where I could be totally me and not a man in black with a white collar, but that didn't mean "inappropriate behavior." The accusation. Who was it? Where did it come from? El Salvador? That didn't seem likely, but it was taunting me. I racked my brain, but had no recollection of crossing a significant boundary.

As stated before, El Salvador's Bishop Romero had once said, *there are many things that only can be seen through the eyes that have cried.* Somewhere in my life I had been insensitive. Someone was hurting deeply. *But me, aggressive?*

The representing prosecutor was presenting a civil case of sexual nature. Yes, life holds numerous temptations for a priest if they are truly among the people and not hiding behind a cassock. An action or word can be misread. Long-term counseling carries danger. Even a short-term intervention has hazards. The confessional format allows a person to enter a small room and choose a kneeler with a freestanding screen divider—somewhat formal, or, to sit beyond the screen informally face-to-face with the priest, which may feel vulnerable to some. Generally, the church leaves this choice to the penitent. With discretion, a good priest might advise a person to use the traditional formal approach (especially suggested for children). Ordinarily, I saw few problems with adults in the face-to-face setting. And looking at it another way, if someone attacked me, I could yell also! Ideally all room type confessionals have a window within the entry door promoting proper behavior.

Summer days passed and my anxiety was rising. Even the routine of five in the morning for prayers and quiet meditation allowed me no peace. A brisk walk and a hardy breakfast did not relieve my stress. I called a mentor and a friend and revealed my burden. He came by my wooded earth home place. We plugged through my life year by year trying to recall any situation—even the ten possibilities enumerated by my cousin-housekeeper (so long ago). Had any of these situations placed a woman in a compromising position? Then I thought of Ann. Why? Only Ann had met me in discreet places, stayed overnight, or invited me into her home when no other adult was present. But I trusted Ann! No, it could not be her. My mentor agreed. However, he chided me for my general behavior.

Within the hour, the two of us began creating a hypothetical profile: Possibly a jealous sort—a person who gets very irritable when they see group attention or individual personal attention given to others rather than...oh my, Irene came to mind. She had worked with my last parish. But it was more complicated. Another situation years ago. I had known Irene before her employment with Church of the Holy Spirit. Was I guilty? I thought about the sermon written by Pope John Paul II. *Our (priestly) sin carries the gravest of personal and social consequences!*

I shall examine the circumstances: It began with a common denominator—sailing.

Irene, a new convert, had never married. She seemed independent. We met at a church conference. Originally from Maine, she had sailed since a youngster. Spontaneously, I shared my dream to buy a yacht. She thought a person needed extensive experience before making such an investment. A lesson was arranged with several participants—the idea sounded safe. There were supposed to be several people, but for some reason they didn't show. Irene insisted we take a course around the lake—and I verified her sailing instruction was excellent.

The next time, a couple did show up along with me and we took another lesson from Irene. This continued until we all felt confident. The couple was great and added a bit of humor to the day. I offered to pay Irene for the instructions, but she seemed insulted by the offer. "Aren't we friends?" she asked. I affirmed we were. She said something about friends spending time together and hoped we would sail again. If I had been thinking of a water buddy, Irene didn't fit that picture.

And then when I saw her at a Fourth of July boating event, she seemed perturbed that I was with a group of people. To pacify, I asked her to call me. We set up to meet on my next day off. That decision turned out to be a two-some, but I accepted it—this was a mistake. When we got out a fair distance, the wind died down—I tried the back-up motor. It seemed dead. I was frustrated and jumped into the water to assess the motor problem. Irene acted like this was all wrong. Her voice got louder and louder and she started shouting at me as if I had planned the disruption. I returned to the boat. My cotton shirt and long shorts were soaked and clinging like skin. I tried to towel them down quickly. This must have embarrassed her. She looked bothered, maybe upset. And being this all happened years ago, I don't remember exactly how we managed the return, but I assume we got the backup motor running, or more likely, the wind picked up and worked to our favor.

Five years following the boating mistake, Irene showed up. Not just to visit our newly built church; she was looking for work. My staff said her general employment record looked impressive, yet personal references were limited—that should have been an alert. But I felt I owed her some assistance. We hired her. It didn't go smoothly. There was subtle tension on a daily basis. And later, she seemed competitive, and yet inward.

As I thought more about it, I remembered that crowds seemed to make her nervous. Small groups were not necessarily an alternative. If I showed affection to anyone, this would launch aloofness—even a child or older person could be considered a rival. Finally, I discovered a solution. I had flowers of appreciation placed on her desk the first week of every month. Irene seemed considerably happier and yet her flexibility and personal skills remained complicated. Unlike the staff person she had replaced (who had gone on to an assistant director position at a different parish), Irene was narrow in her capabilities. We found no alternate position to move her into, so my administrative staff accommodated her. This went on until I retired. Now this is my point of view.

27

Repercussion

The accused. My fading blond hair became grayer. Then the worst day of all: Now I'm informed I can declare remorse and offer payment to the "injured party," or I may challenge the accusation. But this is how it works. If so challenged, a representative prosecutor for the alleged injured party would proceed with a civil lawsuit.

But I would not agree to a settlement. Our diocesan bishop was furious; he knew it would go public. True. There was a small write up in the local Catholic weekly and a short clip in the local newspaper. But I never dreamed it would warrant television—the five o'clock news. That was the worst twenty seconds of my life. I wondered if Ann and her family saw it. I waited it out. Thus far, it appeared many had no clue to what was going on.

First of October, my dear Ann called with the cheeriest voice to see how I was doing; she was referring to my hip recuperation; she had no clue to my legal problems. I hoped I was under the radar. I had hired a lawyer and his proposed strategy was "to draw this out forever." The bishop took matters into his hands and threatened to publically declare me deposed. *What happened to "you are a priest forever?"* My lawyer suggested we submit permission for a hearing in Rome *before* the public court case. (In additional defense, I wish to point out I was *not* being accused of predatory behavior with a minor; I was being accused of predatory behavior with an adult.)

The whole situation felt like a personal vendetta. I had to admit my unpopularity with the last two bishops of the diocese. They had disliked my gender-neutral vocabulary during church retreats and its usage during the service of the Mass. Along with this, the present bishop had indicated his "great disappointment" that I had not arranged a direct endowment of my substantial material assets to the diocese. My lawyer shook his head, "I feel sorry for you." What he really meant: The bishops have influence, just as the rich and powerful—don't ever make these people your enemy.

Ann called again—to re-verify our tradition of shared birthdays; the ritual was secure. I felt relief. Ann has turned fifty-four and I will be seventy-five. She has not a single strand of gray hair and no sign of wrinkling. Her life is balanced—no smoking, only sporadic alcohol intake, dark chocolate, lots of greens and other veggies, two weekly portions of organic beef, plenty of Alaskan salmon, potatoes preferable to bread, fresh fruit, a rare splurge of root beer floats or homemade cinnamon rolls. She stretches every morning and walks every day. No running. Some bicycling. Her latest hobby—writing. She likes doing biographies.

I had suggested we meet somewhere north of the city (far away from scrutiny); DeLuise—an Italian place like something out of Brooklyn. She is there of course; and smiles a bit stiffly after a light hug. Am I imagining this? "How did you know?" Know what? I'm wondering. "I'm writing a true story about an Italian couple." I didn't know. The waitress arrives immediately and we order. Ann places her manuscript on the empty chair next to mine. We're not sitting in a booth so the extra chair is at the table. Ann stares briefly at her food—I bow and say a prayer. This is not our usual way. We had always grasped one another's hands and prayed quietly before eating.

When I look up, she asks bluntly, "When were you going to tell me?" I clear my throat. A reckoning has arrived. "I didn't want to get you involved." Ann has never cussed in my presence, but she mocks it, "What the heck does that mean?" I feel like cowering under the table. Once again, I had misjudged her desire to be present or helpful in my time of need—like that broken hip incident and now my broken spirit situation. "Ann, what can I say? I had hoped to keep the accusation from you as long as possible." That sounded stupid like a man confessing an affair. And she glares at me like reprimanding a student who didn't turn in his critical report.

I start to eat. She changes the subject. "My book is good—the couple are pharmacists who have organized a movement to fight against the abuse and deceptions of the drug industry. Get this, two characters I interviewed said they briefly knew you—something about a sailing class years ago." I take a smaller bite of food and chew nervously. This felt too surreal. How far did Ann's writing and the research go? Was Irene integrated in the story? Impossible! Will Ann bring it up? But I don't want to talk about this and yet...

"Do you have faith in me?" my plea sounds feeble. She reaches for her iceless water, "Of course I do." Then I had to ask, "How did you find out?" She answers, "Was visiting with my sister last night— weeks ago she saw the flash on TV..." I hardly hear the rest of her words because I feel rotten. "Ann—there is no good excuse." She is clamping her jaw and the water waits. My words spill, "I don't know why I said nothing except all women looked pretty negative for a while—but I'm not guilty—you should know that."

She moistens her lips with the iceless water. "But you see how I found out—and that was only because I mentioned you to my sister. Jake, what hurts more than anything, you kept this from me, as if I was among the suspect." My chest feels bound. Of course such could be interpreted—Ann could deduct the lawyer had told me to keep a low profile and not discuss anything with any person who *could be* associated with the accusation. "Ann—I'm sorry." I stop and look around the room. The place is nearly empty, and then, in reaching for her hand across the table, I lamely say, "If this confused woman had seen me with you, she would have added fire to the fire. In that manner, I had to follow the lawyer's instructions."

Ann didn't blink an eye. It all sounded pathetic and desperate. Good Lord, what was I saying? So a better approach, "But I should have said something—will you forgive me?" Her elbows are on the table and her tightly folded hands under her chin. She doesn't reply straightaway. Finally, "Jake, it will take some time— just read my book—and believe in yourself." I try to be light, "Ann you may write another biography—about a Bohemian priest who has a best friend." She laughs. It was the most encouraging sign!

28

Officially unfrocked, latter part of 2006. No longer a diocesan priest. Not allowed to assist or officiate Mass (unless private), or administer the sacraments... My lawyer was still involved. I carried on as normal as possible. I received letters kind and cruel. The priest who had criticized my outdoor Catholic services—whether for students or for the homeless—thought I had received "my due," and stated, "A radical evil person will eventually get caught." The councilman who disliked my liturgical music claimed, "Even breaking moderate rules will lead to a path of destruction." On the opposite spectrum, friends that had traveled with me in El Salvador were very supportive. The woman who once pretended to be my companion for protective reasons wrote a silly but sweet message: "Now that you are an eligible bachelor, I might ask you out on a real date!"

Sister Mary Margaret would re-enter my life and helped me with a small business venture that would raise money for retired nuns with physical needs. It distracted me from my troubles. As for family, their feelings were mixed. My sister was in ill health and refused to talk about the accusations—she said any thoughts of it made her feel worse. My two brothers championed my endurance and assured me of their love and confidence.

When my seventy-seventh birthday arrived, relatives and friends and neighbors gathered at the local church hall. I wasn't feeling particularly keen about this but forced my presence. Ann understood and stayed longer than she had intended. She mixed among the group and subtly supplemented my lack of energy. Very few of these friends and family knew her, and their curiosity was a bit rude. I overheard one person say, "Could she be one of many?" Another said, "Could she be the one?" My deep reaction was a bit delayed. I laughed to myself—did they think any accuser would show up at this occasion? Then suddenly it wasn't funny—I had lost my sense of humor and it would take a lengthy time to feel its return.

Three seasons passed; it was summer. I cared less and less about the mandated "de-frocked status." Externally, it had never been difficult to wear ordinary clothes, and long ago I had shed the black cassock and cowboy boots. Sandals and socks were more my style—comfortable. I sought to stay casual and calm until a dark Monday when the lawyer's office called and informed me that my legal representative had been killed in a car accident. I sent a sympathy card to the law office.

It felt like I would split open. I was losing energy or motivation for choosing another lawyer. But four months later, a business letter arrived with the unexpected—the injured party has retracted all monetary penalties. Soon, paperwork to be signed, and it may all be over! This moment feels like a sign from heaven. I'm drained. The unresolved seems nearly resolved.

M. Schell

123

Part II

29

Presumption

The blue suited man with receding hair adjusted his silk mauve tie. He is not my original representative; he is replacing the woman from his firm. Burn, Browne and Associates is justifying this, saying misconceptions are easily construed. "Let me explain..." following with, "in filing lawsuits, particularly of this nature, unbiased presentation is paramount." Then this heavyset man methodically describes a so-called legal climate, meaning *in mid-western dioceses,* cases like mine do not arise often. So? Now what? He claims most prosecutors are not keen on the "no witness" investigations, especially when it directly involves Christian institutions.

I'm acclimating to the mouth above the tie. "What you or I believe, is not the point; we must prove the guilt. To achieve success the firm has recommended me—a representative that's less likely to reflect an inherent bias towards men." (Justifying his replacement for the woman?) I wanted to say, "We are not talking about men; we are talking about a priest." But I limit my words because time is money, or at least I assumed such, until he states his contingency fees: No charges until the case is won.

I follow his actions. He glances down, and then looks up like owning my attention. "You have been tossed back and forth with the local diocese since the original complaint—in 2003—two years ago." Looking again at the file, "It reads the bishop offered out-of-court compensation, but you required *an acknowledgement of wrong doing* by the accused. The accused would not cooperate. Settlement denied. He claims he is not guilty. Now Ms. Chase—or Irene if you wish—please note—he never states he is innocent. It's your word against his—any *presumption* is defined as the ground, reason, or evidence, lending probability to a belief; it's the legal inference as to the existence or truth of a fact not certainly drawn from the known or proved existence of some other fact."

Ugh! The prosecutor's definition of presumption irritates me to the ninth degree. I feel the warmth in my face intensify; I hate talking about legal stuff. I have worked with people like him. I do not hold great trust in their language. The person before me knows none of this. I want to keep it that way but certain aspects of my life must be revealed, as my present role is to tell the truth and follow instructions.

This representative, who is still talking to me, compliments my general attire: a proper skirt, a conservative blouse, and a light jacket with a small silver pin to my left shoulder. He assures me, "You have the ideal look; we prefer no makeup or minimal makeup." Not difficult. I hadn't put anything artificial on my face in the last twenty-five years, ever since the first time I left Maine. But at this moment, Maine feels very important. I had just visited my family. If I had the financial resources, I would see them more frequently. My family, my sister, my eastern Native American roots—all influence major decisions—decisions like the one I'm confronting.

The man holding my file, sitting behind the polished desk on the fourteenth floor located in the middle of a large mid-western city, has sparse access to my genetic background.

30

Backdrop

My history lies in Maine. It is the state in the Union with the Canadian border on two sides and New Hampshire on the third and the Atlantic Ocean defining its fourth border. (Interiorly, there is the Appalachian Mountain Plateau and the Coastal Plain.) From its earliest days, men have left their families in the pre-dawn hours to take vessels out to gather fish from sea.

My maternal grandfather was a full-blooded member of the Wabanaki Tribe. He owned a wampum belt marked with an eel and a turtle. His biracial blood daughter married a white man who was associated with generations of immigrant fishermen—people who stuck together to help one another until they died. And my sister almost died—as a newborn she had an oxygen deficit. Being the second during the birthing process, I was examined closely. No problems found. So it was a petite woman of mixed origin that gave us life, declaring us daughters of the eastern dawn land— just minutes after Mount Katahdin caught the early morning rays.

Physically, Eileen and I are identical, and my father once stated he got two for one. Memories and photos show us as children together—hiking the trails, scavenging beach shells, sailing and rowing, picking berries near the breakers of the wet pines with our family. To get a clearer understanding, the Chases—my father's English side—lived in the Knox and Penobscot counties all their lives, generations of white blood mixing with indigenous.

My maternal grandmother was part Wabanaki and part French; as a child she was sent to a boarding school, and soon stripped of her Native American heritage. Without any notification to her family tribe—which was required by law—she ended up in a foster care situation. By-and-by she found her way back to her family. (As a quiet person, she never talked about the specific details.) In her adulthood, she took advantage of the tourist growth by opening a small restaurant that offered the traditional clam potato chowder and pastry desserts. Her husband cleaned the fish, her daughter peeled potatoes, and we, the grandchildren, picked the wild blueberries for grandmother's sweet pie.

Our vacation state has a short summer season, as the winters are long and cold. Our home place—our town—is called Tenants Harbor. In the Penobscot Bay area, the tourism industry offers something for all. But located straight north, is the popular Saint George State Park (with both summer and winter activities), and then east is Bar Harbor with its famous Acadia

National Park. For a youngster this seemed like an excessive amount of activity throughout much of the year. Frankly, the summer season would double our population, and that promoted outsiders and crowds. I developed an aversion to clusters of bodies— especially in closed places.

At age eighteen, I was moved up north for advanced education, but the university campus held no improvement—always people everywhere—and I missed my twin sister terribly, even if she is "mentally slow." There was no way she could join me. So be it. Pressure from my sea-faring father pushed an effort to continue at the large land grant education institute. It's situated between two rivers, and a frustrating distance from bay lighthouses, foggy days, old schooners, and the sailing I loved. So while my sister was watching ducks and gulls in the day, and listening to the loons at night, I was stuck behind scholastic walls with books and tests.

Then halfway through my sixth semester, I faced a decision. With one of my grandparents ailing, with my sister needing a bit of oversight, and my mother obligated to help out more at the restaurant, it seemed probable to re-evaluate this four-year university program and return to Penobscot Bay.

At the same time this area was receiving a lot of criticism; state and federal water pollution standards were not being met, threatening eventual closure of the shellfish beds due to high pollution. I knew my grandfather would feel great shame; his tribal people saw themselves as "being" the water, the land, the trees, the animals; and being connected to the original indigenous in Maine, they felt one with the environment. To emphasize the water problem, a report shared by a university professor stated the chief sources of pollutants came from the sewage and effluents of eleven towns, thirteen businesses, and an educational facility, which all caused substantial injury to the market shellfish.

All this negative publicity affected tourism and affected our restaurant. An order arrived for a major cleanup and demanded closure of commercial and recreational fishing areas; my father's lobster livelihood would be in long-term danger—our family and others were seriously wounded by this disconnect from the water. We had a family gathering. After sufficient discussion my grandfather turned to me. "You have to seek employment." I nodded. So in 1966, I would leave the university and move southwest—toward the city. Though difficult, my choice would help them financially.

31

Portland, Maine is a large city with a law school. Thus law offices are everywhere. For me, there was no problem in landing a secretarial position after finishing a technical business course. But living in Portland did not excite me. I adapted because of family: *cooperation, generosity and relationship,* these three are very important in my heritage. In the business world, these values are rarely found. Everything is based on competition.

The man doing my initial job interview would later remind me of the prosecutor with the mauve tie in the Midwest, and neither of the men knew anything of significance about my family. But there were some dissimilarities—the Portland interviewer was mouthy and started me at a low wage. He said everyone has a point of entry until they proved themselves. I was disappointed and looked for a supplement to my Monday through Friday salaried position; all the while my family was becoming more and more dependent on my income.

Like my mother, my petite frame looked delicate, but I was strong and athletic and spent the coldest weekends working in the paper/pulp industry, and the summer weekends, teaching sailing classes in the popular Casco Bay area. This is how I connected to Robert in 1967, a lawyer and married man who twisted my life for endless years. He convinced me to work for *his* department and promised I would "make double" what I was getting at the firm. I didn't realize unspoken conditions were tied to the agreement.

It started with the pressure to dress a certain way and put on enough lipstick to turn a few heads. He called me "Irene" and soon I was running personal errands for him. I was dictating at late meetings. Eventually extended demands turned into arranging parties for drinks and friends, and then, the ultimate weekend suggestion. I was nearly twenty-three and there was no excuse for my saying "yes," though part of me feared job loss if I didn't accommodate his moods. Admittedly, I was attracted to Robert. He was bi-racial himself, though not many could have guessed it. Our indigenous heritage was our primary bond, which now, I do understand.

He liked my boyish leanness and high cheekbones. He favored my communication style—simple and direct. From the beginning with the hotel interludes, he was never severe or bizarre, yet always insisted on undressing me and letting down my long hair, which normally was kept braided and pinned high at work. Not long into our affair, he set up a private apartment. Like many young women, I believed he'd eventually leave his wife. And like many young women, I was wrong.

32

Secrets

My association with Robert meant an elevated work status and the increased salary allowed me to send more money home; as said before—these are my values: cooperation, generosity and relationship. One summer I brought my sister Eileen up to stay with me as mother had her hands full with caregiving. That was the strangest situation. Robert had a hard time getting used to "two of Irene." He soon figured out my sister was simple minded, but couldn't accept our physical likeness. I talked Eileen into changing her style; the shorter cut served a dual purpose: Robert felt more at ease and my sister discovered she could manage her own personal body care.

Eileen had a lot of potential, and that summer we developed it. With much repetition, she learned to prepare meals, to clean, do laundry, draw my tub water at night and rub my back after a long day. We got along well. She loved window-shopping and loved the movies and parks (thirty-three in Portland), but preferred relaxation in front of the TV. She was anxious about going outside without me so I was confidence she would stay at the apartment when I was at the office. It would have been great for her to live with me in Portland somewhat longer, but our maternal grandmother passed, and Eileen's newly acquired cooking and cleaning skills would aid the family restaurant business. In any case, before her return to Tenants Harbor, I asked Eileen not to mention Robert. She loved the idea of a secret.

33

"Do you have any secrets?" Does any person not have secrets? I crossed my legs, which I rarely do. What right did he have to ask? The man in the blue suit, who now has me addressing him as Mr. Browne, seems to believe he can ask *any* personal question. "The more you reveal, the more strategic we can be in your case." Was I going to tell him about the long affair in Maine? Absolutely not.

No one in Kansas City knew Robert, and therefore he didn't exist. I don't believe the details of that relationship to be relevant to my legal case, but the reader could be more curious about it. Remember, this does not come naturally for me—but I will submit. When we were together, Robert revealed his personal problems. He had no children and was not in love with his faded wife, and yet he wanted a son badly, and thus remarked if I conceived a baby, he would leave his wife immediately.

I stopped taking the birth control pill but nothing happened. After being together for seven years—yes, seven very long years—I became sure one of us was sterile. And then his wife got pregnant. And she had a lovely little girl—with Down's syndrome. Robert was horrified. He had not produced a son, and worse yet, he had created "something abnormal." *Something abnormal.* His very words! Associating such a cold remark to my less than perfect twin, I demanded his apology. He acted like a man and did just that. For weeks he bought me special gifts. Sometimes we made love several times through the night. There was desperate play in his actions, as if changing positions or monitoring my emotions and temperature could impregnate me. I don't know what was going through my mind during that Portland period. I was thirty. Did I really want a baby?

It would be a long time hoping for the impossible. Robert became more possessive. Although he conducted himself at work without a hint of our relationship, after a while he got careless. Never flirtation, but noon and lunch meetings together— such was our regular activity. Previously, our private lives had been restricted to nights or weekends.

Then more evolved—health problems, starting with his headaches, very severe headaches. Two more years and slowly we reduced the physical aspect of our relationship. Weekends were spent in loungewear in front of the TV. He set up masseuses to come to our apartment. No alcohol was allowed. Only special fruit slushes and vegetable juice concoctions. At first I didn't mind, but it started to aggravate my stomach and that followed with disagreeable discussions. Despite interventions, his headaches were unpredictable. I started to feel punished for not bearing his child. One night it was too much and I lost patience. I found another place—a new address. I didn't hear from Robert for a month. He wasn't at the office. Someone said he was taking a long vacation. Soon after, I asked for a department change within the firm. Permission granted.

Robert returned. He looked older. His hair looked previously shaven and was growing back. Rumors circulated he had brain surgery. For weeks, he didn't seek me out. I wasn't dating anyone. I didn't feel the desire to. I was back to my original love—giving sailing lessons. In the next couple years, Robert would visit me at my apartment. We had short physical connections, and eventually, a complete disconnect.

The last I saw of him was in the jewelry section of an upscale department store during the winter holiday. I was shopping for something special to give my sister. He looked badly. His color was poor—not easy to regard when covered in a thick overcoat; but his complexion was definitely gray. We had time to exchange a few words before the woman working the counter returned with a small wrapped box with a silver bow. Robert muttered, "Got something for your sister?" I nodded and wished him well.

1978 was not a good year. I heard Robert's brain cancer had spread to his liver and other organs. That year I lost my paternal grandmother and my maternal grandfather. (My father's father had died young.) Now the older generation on both sides of the family was completely gone. Eileen was distraught. All she talked about was death and what happens afterwards and so on. As a family, we had never practiced a Christian religion, so I repeated some Native-American myths and hoped to make her questions go away. For a short while she was okay. Meanwhile, I needed a clean break from everything.

34

The Facts

Mr. Browne pushes his legal notes to the left. "Have you been Catholic all your life?" I clear my throat. "What does that have to do with the case?" The man in front of me winces slightly. "We're dealing with a priest and so any lead to other experiences with church affiliates—even long ago, may influence the present one." He folds his hands. "What I mean is— has any other church representative or priest been inappropriate?" So I'm asking silently—*does having more than one grievance offer more credibility?* I'm shaking my head, "No, only one aggressive priest." And then I remember his previous question. "I'm a convert—I became a Catholic in 1984."

I'm thinking: Native Americans are a misunderstood people. In Maine, we were historically influenced by the white man's doctrine and went so far to call particular white leaders "father"—meaning one who protects (therefore not a reference of specific authority). Yet we were not protected. A four tribal confederacy in the eighteenth century proved the deceit: Lands were contested and divided among the French and English; ultimately, the tribes felt manipulated by the notorious Dummer's Treaty. Still the Wabanaki remained a tribal force until after the Civil War. They would re-organize with other tribes in the nineties to continue the fight for justice.

Sometimes we are called an "invisible people." Throughout American history, treaties were broken and we were pushed off our lands and persuaded to live among the immigrants. For centuries, native and white American unions, Indian and Christian unions, were diluting our blood, and our heritage; I am an example: French, British, and Wabanaki.

Very few people in Maine will admit deep-rooted prejudices. That goes for all sides. My maternal Wabanaki-French grandmother was subjected to white American assimilation until my Wabanaki grandfather married her. Before her rescue, she had been exposed to the very Christianity that decimated her tribal traditions. Carrying prejudice from this history, I had no concrete interaction with Christian traditions as a child, but as an adult it would influence me.

Leaving Maine in 1979, I had headed for Kansas. This was not irrational. One branch of the Portland law firm had extended to Kansas City with a well-paid secretarial opening. The relocation was a viable way to put distance from the broken alliance with Robert. I adjusted slowly, keeping to myself. All sorts of professional people walked in and out of the office. Subsequently, I met Mrs. Juwel with the Legal Aid Society.

Mrs. Juwel was called the champion of foster children in the Midwest. Mentally, I re-visited our foster system in Maine. In 1977 our state had the second highest placement in the United States. This reflected the region's ongoing attempt to strip Native Americans of their rights and identity. Following that, the so-called Indian Child Welfare Law had been passed. My grandmother's experience in the foster system put me on alert. I challenged Mrs. Juwel. Her goals appeared admirable: a focus on relationships, problem solving, and parent mentoring to promote family cohesiveness. I asked if I could get involved; that was one way to confirm it. Since I'm not the outgoing type, my writing skills were put to good use—applying for supportive grants was a compatible niche. So for a long period, I would work one Saturday a month with several cheerful women. They were good people. I never got close to them, but enjoyed the volunteer work.

At the Kansas City law office, I had a tense environment. Another married man had begun making advances with subtle references to good-looking legs and disconcerting curiosity about my personal life. I know I am attractive—with or without makeup. Also, I have a memorable face, and I can be aloof. Social formalities and large gatherings do not interest me. Even dating is hard to imagine. Definitely, I did not need another "Robert" in my life. The business environment of the eighties was pretentious; beneath all, even raw... I considered going back to school—to do something completely different.

I know I have not answered Mr. Browne's question about Catholicism; it is coming.

35

As I considered work or education alternatives, my sister returned to my life. Eileen joined me in Kansas City. We were a few years from turning forty and she was a good companion; the single life seemed practical for us. With her in my life, I didn't need friends. Eileen is this pleasant, relatively pleasing person, and part of my responsibility meant taking her out on regular excursions. She had changed since her stay with me in Portland, and now liked being among others; so I got a hold of a local adult program and arranged for her to work as an "assistant" in exchange for breakfast and lunch and paid activities. Eileen loved it.

Then along came Ruth. The newest employee of the adult activity center took a strong liking to Eileen. She was a Baptist turned Roman Catholic and had a simple way, touching my sister's soul. Using her "Jesus Loves You" vocabulary, Eileen was being won over. Ruth had all the answers to my sister's questions about life and death; only a girl with strong faith could sound so convincing. Soon Eileen asked me to take her to Sunday Mass. There was nothing I could do but go along. Though I was tempted to drop her off, that would not have met our assumed agreement to "joint" outings.

The priest was charismatic—his name was Father Thomas. Once he had worked with the renowned Mother Teresa. He easily won the hearts of people. Still I resisted him. The history of my Native American culture had been nearly destroyed by white Christians, so why would I be interested in a Catholic faith? Then it dawned on me, my mother had been baptized and married in a church. I wanted to hear the greater story. When I called home she offered a few details. After several minutes on the phone, I explained the problem: Ruth's interference in Eileen's life. My mother asked, "Is your sister happy?" And I said, "Yes." And mother said, "Let her be."

Father Thomas's influence attempted a spread like white clouds hovering Maine's Katahdin's peak. His sincerity, his transparency, I doubted. For the longest period I was suspicious. Then it happened. Like a parting of visible vapor, images fell into place. I decided I had not lived a moral life, and Father Thomas offered a path to forgiveness.

In April of 1984, two identical women were baptized. To prepare, we both cut our hair super short. And after, I quit the law firm, and "trusted in God." Within days a position opened up at the diocese—a part time secretarial position, a guarantee absence from flirtatious men.

36

As a "new" Catholic, I confronted my unlikable tendencies. My straightforward and tactless ways were not at all like the historic diplomats and treaty makers from the Wabanaki tribal people. I was well aware friends did not come easily. Father Thomas suggested an upcoming conference to expand community outreach. Who would be there? "Predominantly church volunteers—basically a committed group of people who build friendships based on and through their work with the church." Father Thomas knew I had only part-time employment with the diocese, but money wasn't terribly tight. I had a savings account; so even with Eileen's added expenses, I could consider this conference with its emphasis on "volunteerism." And furthermore, Ruth was offering to take Eileen into her home for the weekend.

The conference was arranged well. There was a priest informally called "Father Jake." He was composed yet vibrant—a white man with Native American allure. This seemed extraordinary. Not a rambling speaker, he chose his words well. He had a steady manner. He appeared to be an effective community organizer. He lined up inspirational people for testimonials, projects were presented;

this was followed by a question and answer format, and then an impressive video with an allotment for meditation and prayer. Afterwards, participants were paired off for a "personality" questionnaire. I was placed with a woman named Carol who seemed a lot like my sister—kind and cheerful.

We all sat together for lunch. Carol knew Father Jake well. Halfway through the light course, we got on the subject of sailing. There was a site called Clinton Lake, a popular recreational area, and Carol said she would take me there. Then Father Jake shared his goal: to own a twenty-seven-foot rigged boat, but he also admitted minimal practical experience. That led to Maine and disclosure: I could teach sailing. Several in our lunch group expressed an interest in taking a rented rig out to water. The conversations flowed. People chatted easily. Common interests. So Father Thomas had been right.

But oddly, I must have misread the group. On the appointed date, the only person who showed up for sailing class was Father Jake. I kept reminding myself he was a priest. He seemed comfortable enough to go out. The wind was good. Impressively he had prepped with a technical vocabulary, so my instruction went smoothly. Steering and tacking are always important, relying on feel and nature, instinct and wind. It was an excellent day.

Father Jake agreed to more lessons and even managed to bring along a few people. I accepted monetary re-imbursement from everyone but him.

It seemed inappropriate to expect a payment from someone working directly for God. I imagined the church didn't pay him a large salary; that assumption was based on my own moderate wages from the diocese. However, in a later lesson, Father Jake brought up payment. It was again clarified there was no charge. He let it slide, but made no other appointments for sailing.

When I look back, I'm astonished by the speed in which the priest caught on; it was like he had been on water most his life. One might even imagine he knew how to sail all along and used the situation as an excuse for something else. What that was, in the beginning I wasn't sure; but my initial reaction to him was quite specific: *He is like a "brother"—not in the sense known by the white man, but in the Native American sense, and that is an honor; he was considered my equal.* I saw him as a trustworthy friend. This was unlike Father Thomas, who was seen as a "true father" in our tradition (which implies ultimate protection).

My new friend never called back. It was disheartening. I played over our interactions. He was attentive and mindful during my instructions—which had been firm, as any instructor should be. Cooperative sailing requires close teamwork and yet he did not lean in or brush against me or speak inappropriately. (I had plenty of experiences of sexual harassment to discern that.) Whether he was with me, or with the group on the boat, he was very alert. Even more so, he seemed tied to the wind—the very strong wind—

like my people who are tied to the land, the water, the trees and animals. In scientific language—you might call it a magnetic pull.

37

Accusation

"So describe that first perception, when something did not appear right?" This was the most difficult question of all. I looked at Mr. Browne and frowned deeply. "A glass of water please?" The blue-suited man nearly jumped out of his chair, "Of course, of course!" He left the room and returned with water, not the cheap stuff in a thin polluting plastic bottle, but a glass container with a nice screw-on cap seal. He set it on a smooth stone coaster close to my reach. I tested my grip; it came off easily. To my lips, a bit too cold, and I let it rest.

Reaching in my side pocket, I pulled out a small notebook. Looking at Mr. Browne, it was time to present the proof. "When I was working at a law firm years ago, I learned how important it was to take notes, to not trust one's memory for recall." Mr. Browne smiled too broadly. "Good, very good!" I opened to the marked middle page. In this little green book all my notes are carried discreetly—notes from business meetings, notes from telephone calls, and notes from a disturbing incident.

"I hadn't seen him in several months; then he showed up with three or four people at a Fourth of July sailing event. We agreed to meet the Monday following—his general day off from his parish. I said I would call him to confirm it. When I contacted him, he agreed. We took the boat out quite a distance, using only the motor. Air movement was hopeful, yet not adequate. We halted the rig but had not hoisted the sails. The wind picked up and then diminished— not much can be done with that. Then it was too still. We were both quiet—a bit awkward, and he looked different today—not at all comfortable and his eyes were narrow and flighty. He didn't suggest we sit back or even wait it out. Instead, he leaned over to restart the motor. But it wouldn't connect. Then crazy-like, he jumped into the water. I yelled at him, 'What are you doing!' Minutes later, he yelled back, "Checking the problem." And I yelled, "You didn't ask me." Then he pulled himself up and over the side into the boat again; his attire was clinging to every body part and he was shaking the water off. *None of this looked like the manners of a priest.* I reprimanded him. He should have asked my advice."

Now I looked up from my notes and clarified, "You see Mr. Browne, I'm the expert here, and even if the priest thought he should check the motor, he had no right to proceed without my input. That's not what equals do. No, he was treating me like a helpless woman." Mr. Browne just nodded insignificantly. His face offered no reaction and I continued.

"Next, he yanked a towel out of his tote bag. He looked angry—or aggressive. I backed off and retested the motor. It started up immediately. I looked at him and said, 'And now?' He answered, 'Your call' but the look on his face was confrontational. He began drying himself *and his sailing shorts went low—very low.* I turned my head and decided we had to go back."

Mr. Browne still showed no emotion. He just led with another question. "Very low? What do you mean?" I guess I had to spell it out. *"He was exposed."* The lawyer in front of me was exactly like Robert in the middle of a courtroom rebuttal. He forced, "Describe the exposure." Corroboration. Now I was mad. I hate men—all men at this moment. "So this is how the others will push me in court?" Mr. Browne nodded solidly. "Exactly right."

38

There were more meetings and more questions, but what seemed most puzzling to the legal representative—from the outside looking in—*why later on, did I take employment under this priest?*

My present rationale proceeded:

"This sexual exposure had happened in '85 while I was still working with the bishop at the diocese, and soon after the incident, the bishop offered me a full-time well paid position. I wasn't sure Father Jake had anything to do with this, but thought to keep my mouth closed. After several years, a higher pay position opened up with a secular for-profit, and I took it. My references from the bishop were adequate and he seemed happy to give me the referral letter. (I wouldn't disclose he seemed cheerful to get me out the door.

"The new situation didn't work out. They were a relaxed people but when the supervisor documented 'Office social skills need significant improvement,' it was unfair and I was perturbed. This gnawed at me. It seemed like my experience with the diocesan organization had not transferred to this secular office environment, so I resigned and took Eileen with me to return to Harbor Tenants in Maine.

"I *could not* get re-acclimated to the small town with its extended wet winter cold and crowded summer tourism. Eleven months later, I returned to the Midwest. It was difficult to find employment. I looked up Carol. She was working with Church of the Holy Spirit and said a recent position had opened up. The roadblock: Father Jake was the pastor of the congregation. I had never issued a complaint of what happened five years ago. Still I thought to explore this employment situation, thinking maybe the priest had changed."

Mr. Browne rubbed his hands and nodded repetitively. "We'll discuss more later. You kept good notes. We certainly have details supporting your case. Like I said previously, we are seriously interested in prosecuting this priest and truth is important." He had emphasized "truth"—I wasn't insulted or defensive; this was legal talk. Interpretation or not, I was reporting how I documented it.

I left Burn, Browne and Associates that afternoon knowing they would proceed with the investigation. Half of my life has been spent trying hard to get along with white people and if I wasn't appreciated *then payback was ripe*. I do think if Eileen had returned to Kansas City, my perspective might have softened. But when all the horrible clergy scandals broke out, I began wondering why I had allowed myself to be baptized—it felt like the abuse of the vulnerable. I'm not necessarily placing me in *that* classification, but I had sufficient reason and motivation to correct my injustice.

I had to accept Eileen was not with me. She had chosen not to return. Perhaps I had neglected her. Maybe she simply wanted to be with our parents—and so she had stayed in Maine. Obviously, I didn't fit in at home any more. This was especially disappointing to my parents since Tenants Harbor was a sailing paradise; with the Federal Clean Water Act, its natural elements were beautiful and protected. Still something pulled me to the Midwest, and when I saw Father Jake again, I finally understood.

This is how it went:

"Five years, you say," he was shaking my hand. It was 1990. For a while the conversation was general and I wondered if he remembered the sailing fiasco. How could he forget it? What if he thought it trivial? I kept studying his face for signs of memory and remorse. Soon he said, "I'd like to show you around, but I have a meeting—Carol will take over." If I had to draw a conclusion, he was very nice, like the first time we had met at that volunteer conference. His friendly movements and his blondish hair, all that was familiar, but why hadn't I noticed his light brown eyes before?

Carol gave the full parish interior tour. She said Father Jake had major input into the design. The main portion of the contemporary building was circular. It was impressive. A huge teepee came to mind. The altar was in the center, so every participant had a full view of the celebrant and the service. All ornamentation was neutral—that is, no white face statues. A good feeling came over me—maybe the priest was apologizing to me—and perhaps others—by *correcting his white superiority.* Maybe he had dedicated his "holy spirit" church to us, the wounded. Then something equally interesting, a small side chapel with limited pews and a simple altar and a lovely picture of a brown-faced woman—designated as the Blessed Mother.

Before a remark could be made, Carol explained the "sister church" connection—the chapel was associated to a parish in San Salvador. I asked the right questions and learned Father Jake and his select group had spent time in Central America. From Carol's voice and her expressions, I saw the admiration. She was just as hooked on the priest as I had been in the early part of our acquaintance.

We exited out of the chapel and moved toward a main hallway with several side offices. Soon I was introduced to Pam and Cathy, who were part of the support staff. They took me through the program that involved a great deal of organized services. Holy Spirit was a large parish with children and youth education classes, adult faith formation, prayer groups, vacation Bible school, community outreach, visitations to the poor or shut-ins, hospital and prison ministry, complex liturgical preparations, stewardship and general fundraising, and on and on. My potential location had an expansive window space, directly across from the administrative office. I contrasted this program with my previous diocesan experience where I had minimal exposure to the broader group as the bishop had boxed me in the archivist section. This larger room was like open space. I could handle this, or so I thought if given a desk and allowed to work alone.

Carol stated the present opening was primarily secretarial. "So when can you start?" she asked. With some hesitation, I almost stuttered, "Could leave my resume with references." I was baffled; apparently Father Jake chose not to have input into this process—he had delegated it. Carol promised to call before the week was over. She walked me out the door and we visited the meditation garden and took in the general landscape. As I departed, the wealth of the neighborhood stood out stronger than it had before. I hadn't asked about salaries, but was guessing it would be sufficient.

That night I stayed with Ruth—the employee from the adult activity center; she had taken me in since my recent return. Being close to my sister last year, she had fair exposure to me; it probably brought forth good memories as she talked several hours. Ruth was now engaged and revealed every minute detail about the upcoming wedding... "You know Father Jake is going to officiate the ceremony!" It seemed everyone was connected to the priest.

Ruth accommodated me for several weeks as I looked for an apartment. She suggested a place not far from hers. This warmed me in a kind way. The young woman was casual and attentive—she had an air of total acceptance as if she could treat the most unusual sort with hospitality. Our time together precipitated some story telling. She was the first person (exempting confession) to whom I revealed my past—that long period with Robert.

"Would you do it again?" A strange question, but I answered, "Possibly—you see he wasn't a bad person." She looked puzzled and replied, "But he had a wife." A sigh. "Ruth, I'm trying to say, he just wanted happiness and that meant hoping I could bear a son." Ruth shrugged, and finally stated, "But vows before God should not be broken."

Suddenly I said, "Like a priest and celibacy." And she nodded. So I carried it farther. "*Should a priest spend private time with women?*" She frowned and suggested, "I would not think it wise on a regular basis." Now I pressed, "How well do you know Father Jake?" Since Ruth knew I had an application in for Church of the Holy Spirit, she proceeded, "Everyone I know accepts he is extraordinary—perhaps he has a unique group of friends, but I think his heart is in the right place—he loves the people of God." I bit hard on my lip, and didn't probe any further.

39

I was hired, and six months into the job had observed that Father Jake delegated almost excessively. This seemed to free him up for multiple involvements, often spontaneous ones. If someone unexpectedly walked through the door, he dropped everything to give his undivided attention. I remembered how that behavior had once drawn me to him. Not for long. I would never say I was jealous of others, but I could say I was competitive. Nothing bugged me more than to be in the middle of a conversation when he would stop and reach out to someone—leaving the assumption we could resume our conversation at another time. Yet none of the other staff seemed perturbed by this behavior.

"So he takes every Monday off?" I asked Pam. "Sure, that's typical—most priests take either a Monday or Tuesday to get in some rest." Carol was nearby; she smiled wide every time "Father Jake" was the topic of the conversation. I let it sink in. Cathy nudged Carol. Then it sunk deeper. I would lay awake at night wondering about the people in this priest's life. I admitted I wanted to be one of the select. It puzzled me. I never had this reaction with Robert.

I never wondered about the time spent with his wife or others—he satisfied me physically and until the latter aspect of our relationship, he was a good conversationalist. When his wife got pregnant, I was OK—basically OK because financially he provided me a good lifestyle, and I had more money to send home to my family in Tenants Harbor. Life with Robert was part of the old way: cooperation, generosity and relationship. I struggled to see deep elements in this priest. To think I had once thought he had the spirit of our people.

In early September, it was unusually cool; I decided to call in sick. I rose very early. Parking my vehicle on a side street, the priest's Monday routine had begun. The rectory reflected a flickering inside like a prayer candle. As dawn broke, fog was still hanging (like my early hours as a little girl sitting on the beach breakers). It cleared. Then I noted increasing movement and the priest exited in casual attire. He got in his vehicle. I followed behind—a discreet distance. Apparently he met a man for breakfast downtown. They sat near a window, so I viewed the interaction easily. That was a long interval. Then he headed to a hardware store—something in a small brown sack was bought. Next he took the familiar route of the years ago—the one to Clinton Lake—where we had sailed. From my car I could see another vehicle pull up beside him. The person slowly got out—stocky with short hair, but not mistaken for a man. She and the priest were removing small coolers and fishing gear from their cars. It was plain what they were up to. I drove back to the city.

On Tuesday, the staff asked if I was feeling better, and I said yes. Father Jake arrived early, looking refreshed as he usually did every Tuesday (unless he had a Monday funeral). We gathered around the conference table with reviews and updates. There was always allowance for creativity. Some of the women had innovative ideas; I usually stuck with the facts. Then strangely Carol asked, "How was the fishing?" Father Jake replied, "We had a fair catch." So she knew what the priest did on his Mondays in September! Once again, I felt left out. What other things did the woman know and keep to herself? It had been an ordeal yesterday just to gather what I did, and she had the information all along. I remembered how Cathy had nudged Carol after I had asked Pam about "Mondays," and now I was seething inside.

40

I kept to myself all week. None of these women knew about "my situation" years ago. They could pretend to be important but I knew a lot more than they realized. And later I thought I had this figured out: though Father Jake shared basic aspects of his alternate life, he never revealed the specific names in those sharing his rest and "pleasure" moments. It irritated me, *that maybe Carol* was another person he socialized with. How many times was she gone on Mondays? Not often. I needed to be realistic—unless—unless they met in the evening hours like Robert and I had done.

Eight months later, Father Jake remarked he had purchased his twenty-seven foot yacht—the vessel he had once talked about. My hopes rose. Did this mean I would become part of the inner circle? He knew how passionate I was about sailing. But the spring and summer passed and nothing. Besides small tidbits about the "cooperative weather" there was no inclusiveness in this new endeavor. Then I obsessed. How could he afford a boat? This was a priest who should reflect poverty—I didn't understand it. This type of Catholic cleric behavior seemed unacceptable.

I needed to talk to Ruth. She and her new husband

were living in Shawnee Mission, Kansas. We could have met at a restaurant, but almost predictably Ruth invited me to her new home. Her formal wedding photo was displayed in their main sitting room. It had been a large event. Her husband was a practicing dermatologist in a medical group and had financed the celebration. Ruth had been an orphan among the un-adopted, and with no relatives, she had relied on his family to create the "perfect day."

Having known Robert those years ago, I could blend in with any socio-economic class, so sitting on Ruth's white divan felt as normal as sitting on the beach. Since the young woman knew my personal Portland history, and my decade of luxury living, I had no judgment of her simple life morphing to this extravagance. But it proved an odd setting to discuss poverty.

"Don't all religious orders take this vow?" I asked. Ruth had only been Catholic for a decade, and yet, she knew the rules and traditions far better than those born in the Faith. "Generally the vows are chastity, obedience and poverty, but I imagine some divergence in particular religious orders." I was thinking about a large sailboat when I continued, "Wouldn't owning any substantial property be against the spirit of priestly poverty?" Ruth nodded, and then said, "I'm not sure about this. You may want to check with someone else."

Feedback is important. She was my only reliable friend, and such credited to my sister. I'm not sure Ruth would have stayed connected except for her self-imposed obligation to nourish and support the people she had witnessed and assisted in converting. This said, she would have been very upset if my backsliding had been brought to her attention. (I hadn't attended Mass for some time.) Dear Ruth always assumed as long as I was working for the Church of the Holy Spirit that I must be a faithful member. Even now, she spoke of God like our primary love. When newly baptized, I had assimilated part of her joy, but during present times, I sensed our bond was fragile; and it was tested when she read a letter from Eileen.

My sister writing her? I had received long distant calls from Maine but rarely a letter from Eileen. The page was passed to me—a nice share. Sure enough, it was my sister's handwriting, but the style and format were more advanced in its thought process. I had no idea my sister could write a proper paragraph. "Isn't it marvelous!" Ruth proudly noted. Yes and no. Here I was getting information secondhand, just like I did in our parish office. I'm not emotional—and yet I felt like crying. Even so, I acted like I already knew, "Yes, she is good isn't she?" Soon I made an excuse to leave—like "I have to pick up some items for the church." And Ruth looked satisfied.

41

Nearing my fifties, my disposition would become erratic and sometimes out of control—the three other staff persons were about my age but had made it through menopause with lighter symptoms. I talked to my sister on the phone—Eileen was having a very disagreeable time also. "You know how it is—the worst part is the night sweats." I agreed with her and then asked, "How are mother and father doing?" I hadn't been home for a while and yet my parents seemed strong and persevering. There was no need to send extra money; both were on government benefits. And Eileen had found a limited work situation in Maine and proved herself a dependable assistant.

Our menopausal symptoms had extended longer than the norm. That's a fact, not a complaint. I'm not the kind of person who feels sorrow for her self—I don't need sympathy. When I hear about "falling into depression"—I have only Robert to relate to, and his depressive attitude destroyed him. Even when my father's commercial fishing job was eliminated, and even when our family restaurant was on the brink of failure, we were able to put together a plan and proceed. My Native American blood, though mixed with white, still flows; it's an anchor. Robert had forgotten how to access his. Not me. Regardless of problems, I am tied to the past. I feel its presence. Grandfather told stories and he imprinted that the white man may try to steal from us, but it's never completely possible, because our spirit is part of earth and it provides for us.

42

The Case

Six months is fast in the legal world. I understand this because I had worked in law offices both in Portland and Kansas City. Burns, Browne and Associates called me for another appointment. It was familiar now. The representative prosecutor in the blue suit—he always wore a blue suit—was still collecting data... *"We need to understand this priest and how he ticks."* Of course by now Mr. Browne knows I had worked for Church of the Holy Spirit and its pastor for a long time. Thirteen years to be exact.

I have already delivered all hand-written notes to the lawyer, so I'm calling upon memory. "Did I tell you about the flowers?" (Robert never bought flowers—he and I thought plants were meant to remain in gardens and fields and enjoyed in their natural wonder.) "No, tell me," the lawyer stated in that monotone voice used when he is puzzled. "Well, Father Jake had this idea that flower deliveries to my desk would make up for his multiple disruptions and his lack of attention to office detail and pacify any coolness I felt toward him—I think by this time he was worried about the sailing incident." But Mr. Browne didn't seem impressed. "And what data supports that?" It may or may not have been significant, but I would state, 'That is my deduction because no other staff received flowers.'"

Mr. Browne nodded for me to continue. "It's vivid now. Pam and Cathy would tease me about being Father Jake's favorite. Then they started to buy me several plants, filling my southeast window. Carol had an allergy to numerous varieties, so she rarely popped into my space. If I needed to communicate I would go to her sterile looking office. Once I walked in and Father Jake was leaning over Carol's shoulder looking at something she had written. The physical closeness looked almost intimate. He moved quickly apart. He pulled up the spare chair and asked me to take it, and added, 'Irene, we need your input...' I don't remember the subject—yet Carol was embarrassed."

"So was the priest uncomfortable or not?" asked Mr. Browne. I liked this type of question; it made me feel like something was being solved. And it deserved a pause. ""Only in his first movement. It reminded me of the boating incident when the motor had malfunctioned and he had jumped into the water. I have watched him closely over the years. His normal activity mode is slow and careful, but he reacts quickly under certain circumstances." Mr. Browne was nodding again. "Can you come up with *more* examples with *specific* reactions referencing detailed circumstances—the more the better."

I'm back to my place. First, I examine my norm.

Spring through early fall is always tied to sailing events or enjoying the public parks. My winter weekends are spent in museums. Other than that, there is a general routine. My cat and I have breakfast together. I pack a food sack and go to work for eight-and-a-half hours, including my lunch break. I am not a heavy reader, so I take in a few good educational programs on TV. Saturdays are meant for personal chores and shopping. I used to go to Mass on Sundays—when Eileen lived with me—but now I choose to take drives out of the city. There is a lot of nature to enjoy, and it allows for recall.

The parish had plenty of social events but I avoided most of them. I never liked the crowded stuff. The few activities I attended were with Ruth. It was with these events I recollected other examples of incriminating behavior. *The priest had been far too familiar with certain people.* He had put his arm around several young elementary age girls. He rubbed the mid-back of one of them as he stood visiting with the parents. He sat extremely close to some of the high school youth, squeezing in on a bench. There had been several young people competing for his attention—and he seemed to go along with it. I *never saw any other priest act like this*, but it seemed to make him popular.

There was a long time when our staff was encouraged to attend fundraisers for the retired religious in care facilities. At one event, there was a particular lady who seemed to receive an exceptional amount of attention; I remember thinking how obvious it was. I had asked Carol if she knew the woman. "Sure, she is one of our recent wealthy widows—a newcomer who is very generous to the parish." Since Carol had access to all information regarding contributions, I trusted this information.

The wealthy lady took a strong liking to Father Jake. She would brush near his side or grab hold of his upper arm. Later I heard she had paid for Father Jake's California vacation. I had no concrete confirmation if she went along, and it was pointed out that the lady was absent from her regular daily Mass during this ten-day period. I got the feeling the staff felt odd about the absence. Carol seemed especially upset. She re-arranged her office—something she never did. However—to be objective, I heard from an individual, that Father Jake had gone with a priest friend. Maybe there was a larger group in California. But something else was most curious.

After those ten days Carol gave notice—she said her grandchildren deserved more of her time. Father Jake seemed to scramble to find a replacement. A man took Carol's place; this was our first male staff person. By now there was some discussion about Father Jake's departure. Then I met his relative; he had been in the main office going over a large white sheet spread on the desk. It turned out to be a drawing for Father Jake's retirement home. Of course I was extremely perturbed. How could a priest vow poverty and live the lifestyle of the secular? There was a rumor a nice earth home would be built near Clinton Lake. I asked

Pam what she thought about it. "Don't priests go to retirement villages or stay with their religious group?" Pam shrugged her shoulders and gave no reply. Cathy had a few words. "Still an exceptional person—look at the man; he will turn seventy soon and doesn't look a day older than fifty-five." (Near my age at this time.)

These next thoughts I will admit to you but never to Mr. Browne. A wave of jealousy overwhelmed me. I didn't like this feeling but I recognized the origins. Boating. Fishing. A home. All represented my childhood and I wanted it back. I wanted it terribly. I could see Eileen and I enjoying our aging years together. My parents would leave us nothing except their spirit; and something beyond was essential. This priest—and maybe others like him—would claim earthly comforts with no right. This injustice ate away at me. I thought how I could attain my ideal. I could be persistent. Experiences with lawyers had taught me this.

43

The Church of the Holy Spirit and the parish had more surprises. Father Jake announced the bishop had requested he extend. During these two years I watched a very gradual construction of the so-called lakeside retirement home. Father Jake was open to any person going out to the site. So my Sunday drives took on new meaning. But the question of "rights" would nag: I learned the land site was the contribution of a benefactress (that wealthy widow). I learned most construction materials and labor were donated. I learned his brothers and sister paid for the furniture and appliances. And toward the final phase, parish members were hosting household gift parties like people do for newly weds. I couldn't believe any one person could accumulate so many friends!

Yet Carol was gone; and she never came to visit the parish office. The man replacing her had a business degree; he was operating as the administrator. He told me, "With the continued priest shortage, the bishop wants to separate out administrative duties and free the clergy to better serve the people." Such was defined as outreach ministry—not just liturgical services, education oversight, baptisms, first communions, adult confirmations, weddings and funerals—but more direct priestly involvement in home visits to the poor and elderly, hospital and hospice, and even new seminarian solicitation. I felt a desperate church climate. Then I reflected. Father Jake had been doing this all along! Carol had been "the administrator" and me the appointed "office assistant." Pam was still the education coordinator, and Cathy still managed the liturgical calendar plus its related programs. Apparently, the bishop had no idea how we had operated our parish.

Before the two years had passed, the Bishop sent another letter for another extension request, as if power could hold Father Jake indefinitely. His parish family would have kept him forever, but the farewell was organized. It was going to be a large event. Rumblings of the bishop's disapproval reached us. I understood why, but no one else seemed to care. The diocese must have been extremely unhappy when Father Jake declared his final day—October 15th of 2002. Obviously, any priest that is in excellent mental and physical form would be expected to carry on for numerous years; but this was not in the written policy—the policy stated retirement was official at 70, and Father Jake had already put in two additional years.

Now let me be clear. I had no positive feelings about the way this priestly retirement was being dramatized. Where was meekness and humility? When a thousand people showed up for his final reception, I was on the verge of vertigo. There was a huge spread of punch, assorted cookies, nuts and mints. A long table held endless photos and other memorabilia. Speeches and more speeches. Testimonies and more testimonies. Toasts and more toasts. It was all too much and I scooted out early. My staff position was secure, but I wanted little to do with these Catholics and their egotistical priest.

While the bishop decried ministry shortages, multiple church abuses were brought to public awareness. *I was so disturbed I followed every allegation.* Part of me was declaring, "I am not alone!" On weekends in the library, I began to research cases—priests who had exposed themselves or committed other unacceptable behavior. There were numerous situations concerning minors, but rare reports concerning adults. So I was in the minority. This did not stop me. My research continued.

After Father Jake moved to his new place, I never drove out that way. If he would not commit to another extension and help his people in need, then he was not fit to continue as a priest. Why should he benefit materially and live a life of pleasure when he had broken vows of obedience (the bishop's request for another extension), and poverty (the flaunting of a private home) and chastity (bodily exposure to me and perhaps others). I saw myself as a crusader, and justice would rule!

With sufficient research and data collected, I had the motivation to seek legal advice. The advisors reflected two possibilities: that Father Jake's actions had either been inappropriate or actually legally injurious. Nearing the latter part of 2003 there was possible justification to go to the bishop. I did not plan to litigate the diocese; I only wanted a specific settlement from the priest—a large settlement. From my observations, it appeared Father Jake could afford it. And I was prepared for a lengthy battle. Such a legal case can be expected to carry on five years. Time was on my side. My people—the Wabanaki tribe—have great patience. They have fought many battles for righteousness, and now it was my responsibility to do the same.

44

Conclusion

When the bishop received my complaint, he "suggested" a resignation from the parish. He worded this carefully. It was to be voluntarily. And yes, I would resign. It would have been difficult to continue with Pam and Cathy, under the present climate, even with my accusation guaranteed confidential. The bishop assured that Father Jake would not have access to his accuser's identification until the first hearing was scheduled. He politely stated there would be a thorough investigation, and when completed, the diocese would contact me.

Twenty months passed and no progress. My savings account was dwindling. I contacted the woman prosecutor who said it would take multiple steps to present the incriminating evidence but she planned to seek a negotiation for settlement. I had confidence when she gave permission to leave Kansas for an extended period. Eileen was ecstatic. "Yes, I'm coming to Maine," I had told her. My sister sounded happy and my immediate image was like a feast: the two of us retiring together near the water. We deserved this. Eileen interrupted this thought, reminding me our parents were getting older and it was important to spend time with them.

When I returned to the Midwest, my case had been moved from the female prosecutor to the man in the blue suit. In 2005 we are closer to the litigation process—this is after two long years of data collection, the full case report to the diocese, and our failed first negotiations. Since our attempt for out-of-court settlement was unsuccessful, a civil lawsuit remains the only option. My lawyers said we had a strong chance and eventually we should win, but the verdict could be challenged with an appeal. Bad news. There could be a stay (or postponement) of a judgment enforcement order—and money would not come in. I could do nothing in the endless months ahead.

In late 2006, the bishop publicly "unfrocked" or "de-frocked" Father Jake. *Looked like the church was not on his side.* Oddly, I didn't consider the emotional effect this would have on his friends or family. My legal struggle was exhausting—why would I be sympathetic? Instead, I focused on the one accomplishment: officially he was no longer a priest. Soon after my parents had major strokes. Both died within a month. Eileen was unstable. I brought her to the Midwest. Now we are back to Sunday Mass.

With the *details* of the case made public, I lost my friendship with Ruth; even with my sister at my side, all contact was cut off. We found a new parish on the Missouri side; Kansas City divides between two states and two bishops, so we were in a new diocese. Living off a small inheritance from our parents, we would plan for next years' early Social Security: Mine decent, Eileen's hardly significant. I am truly discouraged—there is limited money as the case carries on, and I am getting tired.

October. 2008. The world is in financial trouble—nationally and internationally. People are panicking. Then communication arrives. I am puzzled. It's personal. There is an anonymous proposal to *cover legal expenses and provide a check for two hundred thousand with the past put behind*. This is the offer. I may live twenty-five plus years—should I calculate investment and interest and potential monthly income, and weigh that against a possible legal gain? No way! But my heart is beating fast. What if I die soon? Who would take care of Eileen? I wrote back to the anonymous postal box number and asked for a copy of the contract.

The next communication carries the paperwork. This offer does not come from the accused; still the contract requests confidentiality. I can't sleep as I wonder who is the benefactor. For the transfer of the money order, I have only the identification of the mediator. Her first name is Ann. She tells a story, an amazing story with strong elements of cooperation, generosity and relationship—the key elements of my people. So I see peace in the image of a wampum belt, marked with eel and turtle, and like centuries ago, it wraps around me and my sister and the spirit of my grandfather, and all before.

Afterword

Ann proved herself a good writer. She has written several books. One is about the underworld of drug companies, another health care in India, and also a story on Native American culture.

My dear one still remembers my birthday. I try to remember hers. I sit back on the patio chair and watch the birds. I have helpful neighbors, and they are so appreciated. But now there is limited time on the ham radio. I still listen to some stories. I try to enter the lives of people. I see to my needs. I'm aging, and enjoying fresh fish, homemade bread, and wild blackberry jam. I bike some, and walk more, and the breeze ruffles my thinning hair.

On rare days, I think about the woman who believes her interpretation of events—that led to the allegation. Despite her past or present pain, I can't do anything to fix it, given no opening for verbal or written exchange. It is necessary to communicate for the rebuilding of human relationships. Still, there are no regrets of being a man among the people, a man for many causes, a man not afraid, a man willing to take risk and figure out his own way. And in the end, I have adjusted to the pews; it's a different view altogether. But it has a perk—once in a while, Ann is sitting beside me.

Acknowledgements

Presumed Guilt was an unusual novel to write because I had chosen a very natural style with distinct narratives. It appears a simple story but complexity lies within; family, friends, and acquaintances—some who are novelists—have made this analysis. I am grateful for their input and assistance.

I wish to express appreciation to Loren Simpelo who remained exceptionally supportive through my publishing process; a very special thanks to Mariah Hibarger with the Write On Institute as she took up its copy-editing—her enthusiasm pushed me onward. Also I feel indebted to Rev. D. H. Holtschneider, my quoted resource person; he offered important corrections, and his encouragement influenced the final road to publishing.

Reading Group Guide

Discussion Questions

1. How well can we understand action and motive when there exist a cultural or biased divide?

2. Do you know people similar to Father Jake and Irene? What makes these two characters unique? Can you empathize or sympathize with them?

3. How does Ann's role reveal the character of Father Jake? Is it possible she knew him better than he knew himself? What do you think of their relationship?

4. Does Irene's difficult position represent relevant broader issues in our present times? When did you suspect Irene would take legal action against Father Jake? How did you feel about her at that point?

5. Did Father Jake's life represent the Vincentian philosophy? Discuss these elements: The poor must be served...be vulnerable...serve, pray, study, sacrifice...go out among the people...we form each other...mistakes will be made...see to your needs...work must be balanced with rest. Did Father Jake's "personal needs" and recreational outlets present excess temptations or contribute to poor judgment?

6. Why do you think Father Jake is drawn to various women? Can you tie this to the post-Vatican II era and its renewal of the woman's role in ministry? Can a priest have acceptable deep personal relationships with women while being in this world but *not of this* world? What would that ideal relationship look like?

7. Did Father Jake seek to understand Irene's Native American culture and the Wabanaki ideology of cooperation, generosity and relationship? Did Irene's life fully reflect this tribal ideology? In contrast, what were Irene's attitudes towards "white culture?" Define the white man's injustice to the Wabanaki and other Native American tribes.

8. Why was Irene searching for a friendship with Father Jake? Did Irene have more in common with Robert than she had with Father Jake? How did Robert affect her?

9. Ultimately, did Irene help or hinder her family? Did she have an authentic relationship with her sister Eileen?

10. Were you drawn to any of the minor characters like Jake's parents, the elderly mentor at the Saint Louis seminary, the frustrated parish nun, Father Jake's housekeeper and assistant, the staff at Church of the Holy Spirit, Irene's family, Ruth (Eileen's friend), Mrs. Juwel with Legal Aid, or Father Thomas? What were your impressions of Ann's parents and Ann's

husband? Did you have confidence in the lawyer, Mr. Browne?

11. What was your reaction to the diocesan bishops?

12. When did you make a judgment of Father Jake? Compare presumption, interpretation, and judgment. Do you have a personal experience that requires you to re-examine presumption?

13. Was there justice in this story? For whom and why? Are the present secular/ecclesiastical court systems working effectively or ineffectively? What changes would you propose?

14. Do you think your proposal increases communication? Would this change offer a key to forgiveness and healing?

15. In examining the relationships of Father Jake, Irene, and Ann, could "loss" be a core element? If not, what is?

16. Did you discover something about yourself through this story?

17. What scene impacted you the most?

18. Did you feel the author portrayed her main characters realistically?

19. How do stereotypes affect our reading experience? Describe some of your experiences with intercultural relationships?

Questions for the Author

Q: How did this story come about?

Four years ago, I had a temporary debilitating incident. During this same period, I was facing my mother's serious decline, and also feeling discouraged by a directional change in a particular friendship. For emotional therapy, I began writing short stories, one called Presumed Guilt. It took hold as a single narrative voice and that morphed into two voices, and then grew into a novel.

Q: Why write about a priest?

In my life circumstances, I've known numerous priests; more often than not, these continued as positive relationships. In the last decade I became deeply troubled by the upheaval in our religious and secular society whereas power or authoritarian figures wield sexual control or inflict abuse. So with the clergy under continued scrutiny, I believe the character of Father Jake can allow a particular insight, and hopefully, this will encourage a fuller discussion.

Q: Have you any experiences with the court system?

Once I testified in court and it was intense. For the representative person, I observed her anger feeding more anger as the justice system felt manipulated. In another friend's situation, the legal battle dragged for years. During that process, I learned of organizations that solicit whistleblowers (some with financial kickbacks), and other organizations that mold group testimonies toward achieving retribution. Sadly, the goal for truth can be muddled, and additionally, it appears our burdened legal system pushes for out of court settlements. Often this hinders communication and "truth seeking."

Q: What about Irene? Since you are not an indigenous American, how can you authentically represent her?

I grew up near a Native American community; my dad hired men to help with the harvest. There were Native Americans in my parochial school and I have Native American relatives. My multiple travels have exposed me to diversity. When I adopted a minority child, I deeply realized how complex intercultural and interracial relationships are and continue to be. I admit it is audacious to create this character but it's a writer's effort to reflect/search for understanding.

Q: Why did you choose a pseudonym in writing this novel?

In a he said, she said story I thought a pseudonym offered neutrality. By not disclosing my gender, I am hoping the reader feels no authorship bias in the characters.

Q: What is your interesting writing quirk?

I'm not sure I have one! My writing day is mixed with coffee and exercise; I live on a large acreage and like to walk. Equally important, I enjoy song and poetry; it feels calming. If I have a mental block, I leave my writing desk, and create rap or poetic verse; it seems to re-establish my thoughts for the story process.

Q: What is the most surprising thing you have learned from creating books?

Under another pseudonym, I finished a trilogy of lengthy historic fiction. The series spanned over one hundred and sixty years with the last book including an "alternate" history. I was amazed how much research was necessary and how few people wanted to edit this genre in the trilogy epic format. The responsibility of fact checking is extensive in this fictional form.

Q: What does your family think of your writing?

My significant other likes the quiet when I write for a ten-hour period with minimal breaks. As long as I'm deeply involved in a project, my talkativeness is subdued, which makes us more compatible. My youngest adult son is another support person. Whatever I write, he is engaged and interested. He copy proofs, assists with layout, contributes objectively and encourages consistently.

Q: What genre do you like to read?

I'll read most anything with the exceptions of horror and science fiction. When I was young I absorbed historical fiction and non-fiction, mysteries, and the old classics. Through my earlier middle-aged period, I was consumed with political and social issues. Lately, I appreciate memoires.

Q: What is the hardest scene to write?

For me, it's the sexual or intimate scene. I believe less is more. In storytelling, teacher and author, Julie Checkoway, promotes "a balance between authority and involvement, seduction and revelation," and she adds, "...balance the veiled and unveiled, the seen and unseen, the shown and about-to-be-shown." To reign in overexposure and overwriting, one reveals only what is necessary.

Q: What is the most exciting part of the artistic process?

Often my characters come to life in the most amazing ways. I rarely have a preconceived ending. The novel should speak to the writer, and if he/she listens, it may proceed differently than original intent. This can be exciting!

Q: What is the most difficult part of the craft process?

Revision and revision takes patience, and often editing requires putting the story aside and coming back to it with fresh eyes. It may take months or years to complete. There are professional authors who put a book on the market at nine-month intervals. I imagine some geniuses can write well and fast. I create slowly and feel very passionate about the process; the time is often long. This can test one's fortitude. If I get discouraged, I turn to my support team.

Q: Do you have any words of wisdom?

We are like tiny shells on a massive beach and the Internet tsunami of writers will likely keep us humble. Always search for stellar guidance. My favorite is <u>Creating Fiction</u>, twenty-three insights from fiction writing teachers, a collection with an amazing edit by Julie Checkoway.

www.ingramcontent.com/pod-product-compliance
Lightning Source LLC
Chambersburg PA
CBHW021658110726
47902CB00007B/1973